TO KILL A KING

Bailiff Mountsorrel Mysteries
Book Five

David Field

SAPERE
BOOKS

TO KILL A KING

Published by Sapere Books.

24 Trafalgar Road, Ilkley, LS29 8HH,
United Kingdom

saperebooks.com

ISBN: 978-0-85495-545-9

1

1603, Nottingham, England

'I'm getting far too old for this,' Town Bailiff Edward Mountsorrel grunted as he grabbed a drunken youth by the back of his head and rammed his forehead into the doorframe of the unlicensed alehouse shanty. As the young man slid towards the unhealthily stained earth floor, he was grabbed by Edward's accompanying constables and securely tied with ropes before being flung into the cart drawn up outside. He was the fifth, and that was the limit for a cart of this size.

Edward regained his breath, then turned to the old woman who'd been pouring jugs of ale from a hogshead in the corner.

'We'll be back within the hour, and if anyone's left in here when we do, there'll be more cracked heads and more arrests. This unlicensed alehouse is hereby closed down on the order of the town sheriff, and you'll be hauled before the Quarter Sessions if you're still here on my return.'

He was wasting his breath, but it gave what they'd just done a vestige of authority, not that anyone along this thoroughfare had any respect for that. Known locally as 'Backside', the lane bordered the north of the town, but was just outside what was left of its crumbling former defensive wall. It was filled with unlicensed alehouses, brothels, vermin-ridden temporary lodgings and pestilential industries such as tanneries and fullers' workshops that wouldn't be tolerated inside the town proper.

But since it afforded access to the town immediately to its south without the need to show one's face through its more formal northern entrance at Chapel Bar, it was also very popular with those who sought to slink into Nottingham without lawful authority, and for far from lawful purposes. They used to be called 'outsiders', but now the official word was 'foreigners'. There were several good reasons why Edward and his meagre staff of six constables had been tasked with seeking them out, then escorting them beyond the town precincts with strict orders not to return, on pain of being whipped, branded, pilloried or imprisoned.

The first reason was the very present fear of the pestilence re-entering the town from its rural outskirts. There had been several outbreaks of the plague in recent years, and Edward's immediate employers, the jointly appointed Sheriffs of Nottingham, had embarked on a policy of ensuring that the town proper remained an island of isolation from the dreaded disease that began with unsightly buboes on the skin, and could result in a previously healthy person being dead by nightfall. It seemed to be common among those living rough in rural settings, and the forest areas to the north of the town were believed to be a fertile source of the contagion. Hence the need to keep out 'foreigners' who might be creeping south in search of work, or less honest forms of subsistence.

But there was another, and more official, justification for ensuring that the town population did not suddenly swell with unwanted vagrants from its north. The queen who had finally died only a month previously had, just before the start of her decline, enacted two pieces of legislation that were intended to suppress the malaise that had swept the nation. It had been caused by a combination of factors, but its greatest manifestation was the emergence of 'sturdy beggars', 'vagrants' and 'impotent poor'.

Poor harvests, harsh winters, rampant disease, enclosure of arable land for sheep and cattle pastures, and the discharge of thousands of wounded men from the army and navy that were no longer required following the failure of the Spanish challenge, had created a substratum of society whose members were without work, or any other means of providing for their needs or those of their families. Those who were still strong in the arm — 'sturdy beggars' — had taken to robbing those who were not, and they made highway travel even more hazardous. Meanwhile, the weak and starving benighted the streets with their pitiful pleas for alms.

The Vagabonds Act and the Poor Law Act were the confident answers of courtly advisers to the throne. They believed that to be poor was a sin, and that to fail to support the family that one had spawned was an affront to Christian society that must be suppressed before England became a byword for indigent, slothful surrender to the temptations of the Devil.

Responsibility for the suppression of this abomination was imposed upon each parish, of which Nottingham currently had three. The precise means by which 'the lamentable cry of the poor' was to be silenced was a matter for each parish to decide, but one option available to them was the incarceration of anyone caught within a parish that was not their own. Not just those who were desperately seeking work, but *anyone* who might later prove to be a burden on the 'poor rate' that was levied on the more wealthy citizens in order to provide 'poor relief' for their less fortunate fellow parishioners. Since the more wealthy also occupied positions of power and influence within the community, they looked to their sheriffs to ensure that the clamour of those in greatest need was minimised. If all else failed, they were content to see those who might make calls upon their Christian charity forcibly returned to their parishes of origin, or thrown into working houses for the poor, which were little better than prisons.

Back in his room beneath the Guildhall, the town's centre of governance, and with the latest consignments of unwanted arrivals to the town thrown into overcrowded cells on its lowest level, Edward sighed heavily. He reached for his covert brandy supply, swigged a generous measure and reached for cheap paper, a quill and an inkpot in order to sketch out a rough plan for the transportation of some thirty or so 'foreigners' back beyond the town's northern boundaries. Then a thought occurred to him and he rang the bell on his desk, to which Constable Mellows soon responded. Edward looked up from his bench and issued an instruction.

'Send Adkins out to Daybrook without delay, with a message for Bailiff Barton that I will quickly compose and have ready for him.'

He smiled to himself as he envisaged the expression on County Bailiff Francis Barton's face when he read what Edward was in the process of writing, which was a complaint that too many were slipping through his net and finding their way into town. Francis could not control what was happening any more than Edward could, but then he always enjoyed stirring Francis's ire, since it was comical to behold.

They had been friends for many years now, as well as colleagues. They had even shared a house in Whitefriars Lane, across from where Edward had subsequently built his own house when he married Elizabeth. That was well over ten years in the past, but the friendship had deepened by dint of their respective duties overlapping. In those days it had been Edward who served the Sheriff of Nottinghamshire as the county bailiff, with Francis occupying the equivalent town role that was now Edward's. Then they had, by a roundabout process, exchanged roles so that Francis could take up residence in Daybrook, in the apple orchard owned and operated by his bride, Kitty Fellows, while notionally serving as bailiff to the County Sheriff in between harvests.

'It's getting a bit ripe down there, sir,' Constable Adkins told Edward as he poked his head round the open door. 'There's thirty or more in a cell meant for no more than a dozen.'

'Serves them right,' Edward grunted as he reached for the sand-shaker that would enable his missive to dry more quickly. 'When word gets out regarding the welcome that awaits them in Nottingham, they'll be less inclined to creep down here from up north. And when Bailiff Barton gets this stern missive, he'll hopefully put more effort into stopping them before they even reach the North Road.'

2

'Do you feel better after venting your ill humour on me?' asked Francis Barton from the doorway.

'I might say "Welcome to Nottingham",' Edward replied, 'but I wouldn't want to encourage any more visitors from the countryside to the north of it. Have you run out of vagrants to impose on me, and are you now obliged to come in person in order to keep up the tradition?'

'Yes, thank you. I'd welcome a mug of that brandy you keep hidden where I once concealed mine,' said Francis. 'As for visitors from the north, I believe I passed a returning wagonload of them on the road just south of Radford Village as I rode in. I hope they're headed further north than Daybrook.'

'It would serve you right if I had them dropped off at your orchard,' Edward replied as he failed to maintain a stern countenance, and instead rose from behind his desk to engage Francis in a warm handshake. 'How are Kitty and Richard?'

'Richard is proving to be an active handful,' said Francis, 'and even at the age of five he can climb apple trees more nimbly than his ageing father. There are days when he drives his poor mother to distraction, but she's opted to bring another into the world. The child will arrive no later than the autumn, according to Rose, but it's to be hoped that it will be before the bulk of the apple harvest needs to be garnered.'

'Congratulations!' Edward enthused. 'At least we'll have something to talk about over dinner other than the burdens of our respective offices. This should keep Elizabeth happy, since she's currently expecting to add a new Mountsorrel to the list at around the same time. And of course Margaret will treat you like visiting royalty, though Robert still isn't sure whether or not to be frightened of you. As for little Joanna, she does whatever her big sister tells her. But their father regards you as little more than a troublesome blight on the efficient discharge of his duties.'

'If you're back to complaining about vagrants from the forests around Sherwood, then I must throw up my hands in despair,' Francis retorted. 'I have all my constables patrolling the North Road for them, but it would seem that they leave under cover of darkness, and by means of wagons disguised as merchant transports. This is not just a case of the despairing leaving their starvation behind them, Edward — it seems to be organised, but by whom I have no idea.'

'I've been given the name "Josiah Draycott" by several of those I've held in the cells below here,' Edward told him as he poured them both a measure of brandy.

'That would make some sort of sense. The man Draycott is a permanent hindrance to my duties. Whenever beasts are run off, whenever crops are illegally harvested, whenever barns are plundered or orchards raided, the name "Josiah Draycott" seems to linger in the aftermath. It would not surprise me if he were also smuggling vagrants out of Sherwood Forest.'

'Have you never succeeded in laying hands on him?' Edward asked in disbelief.

Francis grimaced. 'More than once. For burglary, fire-raising, even robbery on the Queen's Highway. But never once have I succeeded in having him even committed for trial, let alone punished for his deeds.'

When Edward continued to look back at him with raised eyebrows, he muttered an oath, then continued.

'You clearly overestimate the honesty of our local magistrates, Edward. And not just one — all three before whom he made brief appearances before the allegations against him were dismissed as lacking in veracity. He seems to have them all in his pocket.'

'So he possesses wealth, or perhaps influence?' Edward suggested.

'The latter would be my best guess, since he lives frugally in a cottage on the fringes of Mansfield, along with a doxy from Clipstone. If he has wealth, it can only come from theft, and he keeps it well hidden. It is as if someone is paying him handsomely to perform his nefarious deeds, but I have been unable to identify anyone who might answer that description.'

Edward nodded sagely. 'That accords with what little I have been advised by those I've locked up below here, then returned to their places of origin. Most seem to be from the general vicinity of Mansfield. They all insist that they paid him nothing to be brought into the town, but that it was he who first approached them with the idea that they might improve their fortunes down here. Since in the main they are from the lowest dregs of society, it makes sense that they would not be well placed to pay for his services, and if, as you advise, he is not a man of independent wealth, we must assume that he is fed by others. But why would they do that?'

Francis shrugged. 'If I knew that, I would not be in such low esteem with my sheriff as I currently am. He's sent a despatch to Secretary of State Cecil, complaining that Draycott appears to live above the law, and that it is suspected that someone in a position of authority within the county is playing games with the due processes of law enforcement. As you know, the nation is currently in an unsettled state while we await the arrival of our new monarch, so it is likely that Cecil will wish to present his new patron with a clean slate so far as concerns the machinery of justice.'

He did not need to elaborate. Both men had had occasion in the past to become aware of the machinations of Robert Cecil — heir to his more illustrious father's role as Secretary of State — to all but hand the Crown of England to James Stuart, the King of Scotland. He was a cousin of sorts to the late Queen Elizabeth, and the closest in line for those who wished to see the throne remain in the hands of an avowed Protestant. Cecil had been scheming for such an outcome for some time prior to the death of Elizabeth, partly in the hope of ensuring that the nation's affairs were not at risk of reverting to interference from Rome, which would weaken the influence of career courtiers and administrators such as himself. He also hoped that the incoming James, who was currently on his way south to claim his throne, would remember with generosity the service of the man who had all but presented him with it.

'Did your master also apprise Cecil of the manner in which these recent laws to suppress the poor were being flouted?' Edward asked.

'That also, but it would help if your two could be prevailed upon to make similar approaches to London,' Francis replied. 'We may have the source of our authority divided between three office holders, but in reality theirs is a shared problem.'

He was reflecting on an issue with which both bailiffs had been contending for as long as they had been in parallel offices in adjoining jurisdictions, and one that frequently threatened to get in the way of effective law enforcement. The County of Nottinghamshire and the Town of Nottingham each had, for historic reasons, their own sheriff who represented the monarch in the preservation of law and order. As if this did not present enough potential for division, territorial rivalry and blame-casting, Nottingham by tradition had two sheriffs, who did not always see eye to eye on how matters within their jurisdiction should be managed. They were elected annually, and in the experience of both Edward and Francis, it was well into the second half of their joint year of office before they could be tactfully nudged into speaking with one voice.

The two currently giving Edward his orders — William Littlefare and William Hynde — had only been in office for the past month or so, but it seemed hopeful that the town could look forward to a firm, united approach to the suppression of disorder within its boundaries. For Francis in the county, there was only one man to whom he was answerable — William Rayner of Arnold — but he had, during his first few weeks in office, displayed unrealistic expectations regarding Francis's capacity to hold down a largely rural and widely dispersed populace.

'We shall see what support we might expect from London, once Master Cecil has ceased fawning over our new king,' said Francis. 'If rumour be accurate, Cecil has at last found someone to order him around who is little taller than he is, which is knee-high to a grasshopper.'

Edward chuckled. 'He would have your head to hear you say that. And Elizabeth will have my head if I return late for dinner. She is of course not expecting you, but I have no doubt that at least two of my children will persuade her that your return to our hearth is a blessing from God.'

Edward's prediction proved accurate as they approached the porch entrance to his house, and a child whose height exceeded that to be expected for a ten-year-old came racing out. She hurled herself at Francis with a joyful shout. 'Uncle Francis! It's been far too long! How are Aunt Kitty and little

Dickon? You *must* bring them back to visit! Promise that you will?'

'Inside, young lady!' called a stern voice from the threshold, as a red-faced lady in her mid-thirties appeared in the open doorway. Elizabeth smiled at Francis, and cast a sideways glance at her daughter Margaret as she raced back into the house to announce to her brother and younger sister that they had a welcome visitor.

'I need no guard dog to advise me when Francis Barton approaches my door, for as long as Margaret Mountsorrel resides here,' said Elizbeth. 'What brings you here, other than the desire for a free meal?'

Francis chuckled. 'That is excuse enough, surely, given the excellence of your board? But in truth I am here at the invitation of the bailiff to the Sheriff of Nottingham, as penance for what he deems to be my dereliction of duty.'

'Did he mention his own dereliction of duty to his family?' she asked, directing a frown at Edward. 'It was bad enough when he at least had the excuse of needing to wander into the county in order to discharge his duties, but since he transferred to the town he seems to regard dinner as something he can foreswear almost daily. He only returns to consume a supper of a size that would fuel an entire company of foot soldiers. But come in, and bring my husband with you.'

As they sat around the dinner table, with the housemaid Meg moving back and forth with platters of dried fish, cheese, fresh manchet loaves, fruit and jugs of a thin local cider, Francis answered Elizabeth's questions regarding his family. 'Kitty enjoys the best of health, thanks to her sister Rose's knowledge of which potions may safely be brewed from the plants that surround our humble home. Kitty herself assures me that she remains happily married, and her only distraction is a very active five-year-old who can climb every tree in our orchard, and can hide himself in our fruit barn with a skill that would do credit to any highway footpad.'

'Francis advises me that there will shortly be another little Barton to occupy his attention,' Edward added, 'and I took the liberty of advising him that it will be assured of a playmate from the Mountsorrel brood of approximately the same age.'

Elizabeth looked down ruefully at her distended stomach, reddened slightly and addressed Francis. 'Edward *does* return home occasionally, and his appetite is not always just for food. But it is good to learn that marriage has been a happy condition for you, Francis, since for some years we believed that your interest was only in lonely widows seeking temporary attention.'

'Those days are behind me,' Francis said, 'thanks to your husband going to the assistance of a wisewoman from Papplewick who just happened to have a younger sister in need of a man to assist with her apple harvest.'

'It's good to know that Rose is still in this world,' Edward said, recalling the circumstances in which he had disobeyed an order from the sheriff to whom he was answerable at that time. Instead of having Rose Middleham taken up and hanged as a witch, he had given her safe escort to the orchard property of her recently widowed sister Kitty, whose fulsome charms Francis had found impossible to resist. 'Rose must be of some age by now,' he added.

'She is approaching fifty years of age, which she will admit after imbibing too much of her own elderberry wine. But given her knowledge of simples, natural cures and the healing properties of every plant known to mankind, she seems to possess the skill to preserve her life forever. She certainly keeps Kitty and I in fine fettle, and has already begun passing on her physick to young Richard, who may well become a herbalist or apothecary to royalty one day — who knows?'

'Speaking of royalty,' Elizbeth put in after giving Robert and Joanna permission to leave the dinner table, while Margaret still clung to Francis's arm like a limpet, 'what news is there of the coronation? Does England have a new king, or are we destined to endure years of civil strife?'

'There is word in the county that the Scots king is progressing south in order to claim Elizabeth's crown,' Francis told them. 'I have been advised by my sheriff that I must ensure that peace reigns throughout the villages, and that the North Road is clear of footpads and the like. Seemingly our new monarch is accompanied by many nobles from his own Scottish court, and the pickings would be rich, were they to be attacked as they pass through the Sherwood glades.'

'Surely, if King James is eager to reach London in the shortest time, he will take the shortest route,' Edward argued. 'This will take him by way of Newark, and nowhere near Sherwood, so you need have no concern that his party will be set upon.'

'So it is to be hoped,' Francis agreed, 'since as you and I have discussed, the forest is no place through which to journey these days with one's purse loaded. It is full of cutpurses and assorted vagabonds with no other means of survival than robbing those more fortunate than themselves.'

Elizabeth looked accusingly at Francis. 'I hope that your reason for travelling into town was not to involve my husband in some hazardous scheme that could place his life in danger. If these malcontents of whom you speak are dwelling under the dense cover of Sherwood, then it is *your* duty to rid the county of them, not Edward's.'

'That's not why he came to town,' Edward told her. 'But his difficulty in ridding the outlying areas of those whose misery makes them dangerous is adding to *my* difficulty when someone with an evil agenda inflicts them on the town. Which is why when you receive a response from London, Francis, I wish to be advised. And if they send a person of standing and authority, I wish to be included among those who make representations to them.'

3

Edward paced nervously up and down the narrow vestibule to Sheriff William Hynde's town house in Halifax Lane. It was the house he occupied when in town in connection with his garment business, and was best described as small but convenient. So small, in fact, that Edward could hear the low hum of two men conversing on the other side of the wall to the front parlour into which he would shortly be admitted. He had no doubt about why he'd been summoned this early on a sharp spring day, and he could hazard a guess as to the identity of the man with whom Sheriff Hynde was in conversation.

He heard a door being opened, and from memory he knew that it was on the other side of the parlour, and communicated directly with the steward's pantry. He heard heavy footsteps crossing the wooden floor in the front parlour, the door of which was then opened to reveal the lugubrious face of Hynde's steward, Anthony Pilgrim.

'My master bids you enter,' he told Edward.

Edward braced himself as he strode into the chamber with what he hoped was a confident air. As he'd anticipated, the other man in there with William Hynde was his joint sheriff, William Littlefare, and both men were expressionless as Edward was instructed to occupy the standing space before the table at which the two officials were seated, mugs of ale and a salver of wafers on the table in front of them.

'Why do you think we wish to speak with you?' Hynde asked in his customary pompous manner. Edward was about to reply when Hynde did so for him. 'It's about the outrageous burden being imposed on the town as the result of all these idle poor being allowed to lurk within its parishes. They claim relief from the Poor Fund that is compiled from the impositions it is necessary to make upon our more worthy citizens, in order to subsidise the fecklessness of those whose only effort is in siring whelps for whose welfare they cannot provide.'

Edward opted for silence, which clearly irritated Hynde.

'Well?' the sheriff demanded.

'I'm sorry, sir,' said Edward as he ground his teeth in resentment. 'I did not recognise your words as constituting a question.' From the corner of his eye he noted the smirk on Sheriff Littlefare's face, and his hopes rose slightly as he continued. 'May I make so bold as to infer that you are asking what steps are being taken to minimise the burden imposed on the parish poor levy by those who enter the town looking for work and succour?'

'You may,' Hynde snarled. 'So what *are* you doing about it?'

Edward sighed heavily. 'We scour the lower establishments in the town — particularly those that have been allowed to spring up along Backside — and daily we collect all manner of vagrants and ne'er-do-wells who have recently arrived in Nottingham, and have no legitimate business here. We cast them into the Guildhall cells, then take them back out beyond the northern boundary with a threat that if they are caught returning, they will be brought before the magistrates and branded, whipped, or pilloried.'

'And *do* they return?' Hynde demanded.

'It is not always easy to determine, since they assume different names. There have been several, but the attitude of the justices seems to be that unless we can prove they have returned after a warning, they will not order any condign punishment.'

Sheriff Littlefare tutted, but Hynde was more vocal.

'This is totally unacceptable! The sooner we have a secure and permanent place to lodge these leeches, the better! The law entitles us to confine them on their *first* attempt to impose on our Christian charity, rather than allow them to bounce in and out of the town!'

'How go the plans for the proposed Poor House?' Edward asked, in the hope of reducing the heat of the conversation.

Hynde smiled for the first time since Edward had been in his presence that morning. 'We are almost ready to open its doors, God be praised. The Hospitallers from whom we acquired "St John Baptist", as they called the place, had created a whole series of chambers in which the sick and dying might be ministered to by the holy brothers. It was a simple task to convert them into dormitories in which the indigent might be accommodated and fed, while repaying our charity by picking oakum. But there is an ongoing dispute regarding who should incur the expense of overseeing it. It lies within the parish of St Mary's, but those responsible for the administration of St Peter's and St Nicholas's are demanding the right to send their vagrants there, without contributing anything towards the cost thereof. There the matter rests until we can obtain an agreement between them, a matter on which the Town Corporation seems to be dragging its feet.'

'And in the meantime, from what you can report,' Littlefare added, 'these foreigners come and go at will, surviving as best they can by thieving, whoring, swindling and the like. Has there been no effort by your counterpart to contain them within the county?'

Edward nodded. 'I have, in the past few days, been in discussion with Bailiff Barton regarding how we might stem the tide, but he advises me that it is not a case of isolated and desperate men seeking a means of sustaining their families, but an organised trade by a man from Mansfield we have identified, but whom the magistrates seem reluctant to punish.'

'Then we must prevail upon Sheriff Rayner to do better!' Hynde said to Littlefare, who nodded, then looked back at Edward.

'If you could apprehend the man of whom you speak, and have him brought before the town justices, you believe that this invasion of the destitute and desperate would cease — is that what you are assuring us?'

'It might,' Edward agreed, 'and it would certainly be preferable to sitting helplessly by while the town becomes the chosen dumping ground for those less inclined to obey the law.'

'Then you and the county bailiff must combine your efforts in locating this man and locking him under the Guildhall,' Hynde urged him. 'Do you at least have a name?'

'Draycott,' Edward replied. 'Josiah Draycott. As I previously advised, he resides in the general area of Mansfield, but there is no evidence that he ever enters the town in person. His "customers", if I may call them that, although we are not aware that they pay for his assistance, are brought in by wagon under the cover of darkness. They sneak into the many stews and hovels along Backside, so as to avoid being spotted as they pass through Chapel Bar.'

'This must stop forthwith!' Hynde insisted hotly. 'Do the job for which you are amply rewarded, join forces with Bailiff Barton and stop this pernicious trade in human misery! That will be all.'

Edward returned to his room in the Guildhall in a foul humour. His constables were accustomed to reading his mood from his face, and kept well clear of him until they were obliged to convey the message that had been delivered by fast horse while Edward had been meeting with the town sheriffs. Senior Constable Durward all but crept into Edward's presence as he was muttering over the list of those to be transported back out of the town on the daily cart run, and handed him the single sheet that had been unsealed when it arrived. Edward looked up, murmured his thanks to Durward, and unfolded what Francis had written:

I expect the arrival of someone sent by Cecil by sunset today. You wished to be advised when this was to happen, so consider this my payment for an excellent dinner.

Edward returned home only briefly, to advise a sour-faced Elizabeth that he was departing immediately for Daybrook and would probably not return until the following day. He then rode to the substantial house, financed by several successful apple harvests, that Francis and Kitty had constructed for their life together. The sun's final rays were disappearing behind the steeple of St Mary Magdalene Church in Hucknall, to the south-west, as he slowly dismounted. Then he became aware of a furious argument between two men in the front doorway to the house.

One of them was Francis, who was being held back by Kitty. He paused as he saw Edward approaching, and explained the reason for his anger.

'This oaf, who claims to serve the Secretary of State, has the temerity to insist that Kitty and I give up our bedchamber — the best in the house — for his poxy servant over there, the one stabling his horse!'

The man looked pleadingly towards Edward, seemingly hoping for his intervention. 'I am Thomas Dalrymple, clerk to the Secretary of State, and if this buffoon would stop haranguing me for long enough to let me explain…'

'Explain nothing!' Francis bellowed. 'There is no man on God's earth who would persuade me to give up my bed for some hobgoblin of a servant. So get yourself gone, regardless of your business!'

'Softly, Francis,' Edward urged him as he stepped closer in the hope that he could get between the two men before punches were thrown. 'We asked for guidance, and perhaps some assistance, from London, and this is the man they sent. We should at least hear what advice he brings.'

'Not me — him!' Dalrymple replied as he nodded towards the short, swarthy man who was hobbling towards them as fast as his bent spine permitted.

Edward froze in fear, and it was several moments before he was able to utter a word. 'Dear God, Francis, your mouth will one day get you hung, if it hasn't just done so!' he exclaimed. 'The man you called a "hobgoblin" has more right to occupy your best room than any man in England, other than its incoming king. Even then it will be far inferior to what he's used to. Bend the knee, and offer a most ingratiating and humble apology to Sir Robert Cecil, Secretary of State to King James.'

4

Two hours later, following several grovelling apologies from Francis that were grudgingly accepted by Robert Cecil, the four men finished a hearty meal served by Kitty. They also enjoyed several jugs of Rose's elderberry wine, and she surreptitiously slipped a handful of herbs into Cecil's mug in order to relax his mood. The men then sat in front of a roaring fire, and Cecil opened up the conversation.

'I diverted at Gainsborough from my progress south, accompanying our new king, having received intelligence from Dalrymple of certain matters here in Nottinghamshire. I knew, of course, from our previous acquaintance, that Master Mountsorrel served as the county bailiff. But I understand that he has transferred to the town since our last encounter, and that matters in the county are now the responsibility of Master Barton, whose formal acquaintance I made but two hours ago. If you offer me one more cringing apology for your crass stupidity earlier, Master Barton, I shall be obliged to reconsider whether you possess the wit to be involved in these matters.'

'I can speak for him, my lord,' said Edward. 'He's an oaf, but a loyal one.'

'It is precisely that quality that I shall be relying on from both of you when I disclose what it is I require from you,' Cecil replied as he nodded towards the closed door of the comfortably furnished living chamber. 'Can we be sure that we are not in danger of being overheard?'

Francis got to his feet and walked to the door, which he pulled open with a dramatic flourish to reveal an empty hallway beyond. Then he closed it again and regained his seat as Cecil gave a satisfied nod, then turned to Edward.

'Several times in the past, either myself or my father had occasion to bring to your notice the existence, on an estate in a neighbouring county, of a young lady of high birth.'

'You refer to Lady Arbella Stuart, who resides with her grandmother in Hardwick Hall?' Edward asked.

Cecil inhaled sharply. 'Even with a heavy oak door between ourselves and inquisitive ears, it would be better simply to refer to her as "the lady", although you have accurately identified her. She is, you will recall, cousin to the gentleman who I have escorted south from the Scottish border. This would in itself be a cause for her to be afforded considerable favour, but unfortunately she is of the Catholic persuasion.'

'Our new king regards her as a challenge to his throne?' Edward ventured.

Cecil shrugged. 'Would that he did, then I would not have had cause to deviate from my journey south. Should it be demanded of you, you will say only that you were of the belief that I was visiting distant family, although there are none such in this part of the realm. But I digress. Why is it, think you, that the incoming James will not act against "the lady" in question, even when advised that she may be plotting against his throne?'

When it fell silent, Cecil sighed, refilled his mug and launched into a history lesson.

'You recall the fate of James's mother, the Scots Mary?'

'She was finally executed some years ago, on the order of the late queen,' Edward recalled.

'On the *order* of Her Majesty, certainly,' agreed Cecil, 'but at the urging of my father, who fell from favour when Queen Elizabeth regretted her decision to sign the death warrant. She had wavered for years, reluctant to have the woman executed because of their relationship as cousins, even though plots to have the Scots Mary usurp Elizabeth had been bedevilling the nation for years.'

'And our new king, the son of this traitorous woman, has similar scruples regarding "the lady" we are discussing?' Edward asked.

'You have the nub of it,' Cecil confirmed. 'Although James was only a small child when his mother went under the axe, he believes her death to have been unjust, and that she was simply a silent and unwilling object of the treasonous ambitions of others. He is reluctant to inflict the same injustice on his own cousin, who, he has persuaded himself, is an innocent lamb. He believes her only failings are listening too closely to the twittering of her wealthy but now ageing grandmother, the formidable Bess of Hardwick, and following the Popish faith in which she has been raised.'

'And you know different?' Edward prompted him.

'I know not to what extent the woman encourages treasonous plots being hatched in her name, but I *do* know that their aim is to put another Catholic queen on England's throne.'

'So you cannot denounce her directly?' said Edward.

Cecil shook his head. 'Indeed I cannot, nor will His Majesty be persuaded by those who will form his Council of State that he should be doing more to smoke out Jesuits, secular Catholics, secret agents from Spain and others who plot his downfall before he has even been crowned.'

'And what is it that you require of us?' Edward asked cautiously. 'Clearly, if you cannot oppose the lady and her supporters openly, you must do so by underhanded means. Is that why you have taken time to meet with us?'

Cecil lowered his voice. 'Dalrymple here can apprise you of those matters that have been vouchsafed to him in confidence, but that same confidence must be honoured by yourselves, do you understand? What you are about to learn is only in order that we may engage you to seek out further information, with particular reference to a plot that we believe is already well advanced to seize our new king and replace him with "the lady", whether or not she desires it. So listen carefully and say nothing until Dalrymple has given you such intelligence as he possesses on the matter.'

Dalrymple's voice was even lower than Cecil's as he all but whispered what he had to disclose. 'You must first of all be advised that within what might be termed the "Catholic community" here in England, there are deep divisions. The dominant party, and those with the closest links to Rome, are still the Jesuits. They are led by a zealot called John Gerard, who escaped close custody in the Tower some years ago, and has thereby become a hero to those who follow him, who in the main are more concerned with the integrity of their faith than they are with any political power. They have hopes that James can be persuaded to be more tolerant of the Roman Church and all its trappings because it was the religion of his mother, the Scots Mary to whom Sir Robert referred earlier. Although raised as a Protestant, James is suspected of having Catholic sympathies. Therefore, those who still regard the Pope as their true leader are hoping for greater tolerance, and in particular a reduction in those constraints imposed by the former queen upon the hearing of the Mass and other Catholic religious observances.

'The Jesuits are not, however, the only Catholic association in England. There is another group, which for convenience are dubbed the "secular clergy". They are priests in the Catholic fold, but not so deeply entrenched in their blasphemy as the Jesuits, who regard them with some disdain. To put the matter more bluntly, there is conflict between the two groups, although the leader of the secular group, a man named George Blackwell who delights in the title "Archpriest of England", keeps regular contact with an associate of Gerard's called Henry Garnet, who is the head of the Jesuit faction here in England.' Dalrymple noticed the glazed look on Francis's face, and asked, 'Have I succeeded in losing your attention, Master Barton?'

'No,' Francis replied uncertainly. 'It is just all these names that we are required to absorb.'

'There are many more to come,' Cecil replied testily, 'so simply keep at the forefront of your brain the two names "George Blackwell" and "Henry Garnet". This may assist with what you have yet to learn.'

'Why is that name "Garnet" familiar to me?' Edward asked.

Cecil smiled. 'There is hope yet. Henry Garnet was educated in Nottingham, at the grammar school of which his father was master for some years. And there is a further local connection of which you will learn shortly, if Dalrymple is allowed to continue.'

Edward and Francis fell silent, and Dalrymple once again picked up the narrative.

'We have these rival groups, then — Garnet, and behind him Gerard, on the one hand, and Blackwell on the other. They are at odds regarding how James may be approached in order to secure greater tolerance for Catholics within the realm. You have absorbed that much?'

Francis and Edward nodded, and Dalrymple continued.

'I have recently been visited by Blackwell, who is concerned that the intemperance of certain secular priests who are answerable to him may have led them into a plot against King James. They even went so far as to attempt to recruit Gerard into their schemes, and it was he who reported to Blackwell what his minions were about. I might say, at this stage — although you must guard this knowledge on pain of death — that we have let it be known to Gerard and Garnet that we shall not proceed against them for as long as they continue to pass on to me, or my staff, what they may learn regarding these plots.'

'They plot to assassinate the new king?' Edward asked anxiously.

'We believe that this may be their ultimate ambition, should they fail in their attempts to gain greater tolerance of Catholic observances,' said Cecil. 'At the very least it is believed that they may seek to seize him and hold him to ransom until reform measures have been mandated by the proposed new Council of State, which is likely to contain many leading Scottish nobles who are travelling south with James. This in itself has become a bone of contention with many English nobles who were hoping for preferment.'

'But at all events, their preferred monarch will be "the lady" to whom we are referring, and her presence a short distance across the county boundary in Derbyshire is what brings you here?' Edward asked.

'It may come to that, but for the moment your proposed quarry will be much closer than that, and within the jurisdiction of the Nottinghamshire sheriff.'

'Hence the need to involve me?' Francis asked eagerly.

Cecil gave him a sour look. 'You have already demonstrated your impulsiveness and tendency towards rash outbursts. I must admit that when I first learned you are now the bailiff for the county, my heart sank.' He glared at Edward. 'Nor was I pleased to learn that your duties now confine you to the town,' he added. 'However, the absence of Master Mountsorrel from the county these past few years may well serve our purpose.'

It fell silent until Cecil asked, 'Do you remember the occasion upon which you were sent into Leicestershire at the behest of my father, in order to gain intelligence regarding the activities of a treasonous organisation known as "The Brotherhood of the Blood of Christ"? As I recall, you acquitted yourself with distinction while posing as a strolling player.'

'And I nearly got myself killed,' Francis muttered, but Cecil continued as if unconcerned by that.

'I wish you once again to adopt a character that is not your own,' he informed Edward, whose blood grew cold. On the former occasion, he'd been reunited with his birth mother, only to have her snatched from him by a murderer. He was still grieving her loss.

'Am I to be a strolling player again?' he asked resignedly.

'No, Master Mountsorrel,' said Cecil. 'This time, you will be a vagrant whose only recommendation is his skill with a sword. But we are getting ahead of ourselves, and if Dalrymple will permit me to take over his narrative, I can explain what I have in mind.' Dalrymple nodded his agreement, and Cecil asked, 'Are you familiar with a place called Ollerton, by any chance?'

'We both are,' Edward replied with a nod towards Francis. 'It lies to the north of here, on the other side of Sherwood Forest, as the land opens out near the county boundary at Bawtry.'

'Excellent,' Cecil muttered. 'Because at Ollerton resides the man whose acquaintance I wish you to cultivate. His name is Sir Griffin Markham, and he is a secular priest in the faction presided over by George Blackwell. It was he who foolishly sought to recruit John Gerard. This led to Henry Garnet —

31

through George Blackwell — alerting us to a possible plot against James.'

'Tell me more of this man Markham,' said Edward.

'He is a Catholic, and a very bitter one, who was banished from court by Elizabeth some years prior to her death, for reasons that remain obscure,' said Cecil. 'Since that time he has taken his bitterness and feelings of rejection around the nation, pouring out his venom to anyone who will listen. By this process he fell in with a man called William Watson, who is another secular priest, and one violently opposed to the Jesuit faction, believing that they are in league with Spain in order to restore a Catholic to the English throne.'

'But surely that is something desired by *all* Catholics?' Edward objected.

'Indeed, but you forget the rivalry of which Dalrymple spoke between the Jesuits and the secular priests. It is the latter who wish to be the means of placing "the lady" on the throne, thereby acquiring positions of high office.'

Edward nodded. 'So this man Markham has formed an alliance with this other man Watson?'

'Indeed,' Cecil confirmed, 'and many more besides him, some of them ennobled. For example, there is Thomas Grey, Baron Grey de Wilton, who is actually a Protestant by inclination, but he is one of those who resent what they anticipate will be the preferment of Scottish nobles at the English Court. But there are others among the nobility who we believe to actually be in the pay of Spain; they work to return England to the governance of Rome.'

'No more names, I pray!' Edward complained. 'My head is all but exploding with them. Can we not concentrate simply on this man Markham, who is to be my main target?'

'Yes, indeed,' Cecil replied. 'I hope you will forgive me when I say that yours is one of the backgrounds on which we keep information in my office in Westminster. From this I have learned that you were once in the military service of the Earl of Leicester.'

'Indeed,' Edward confirmed. 'I was in his Trained Band at Tilbury when Her Majesty addressed us ahead of the anticipated arrival of the Armada.'

'I will not pretend that Dudley and my father enjoyed a warm relationship, because they did not,' Cecil admitted, 'but at least he was capable of leading men, which is more than could have been said of his godson Essex, who we executed for treason two years ago. But I digress again — forgive me. It was your experience as a man at arms that put me in mind of you when I was advised of the gathering of vagabonds in Sherwood Forest, and the problems that they were causing for the town.'

'It's good to know that my complaint actually reached you,' said Francis, 'since we are most discomforted by the seeming reluctance of our local magistrates to do anything about the man Josiah Draycott, who seems to be behind it all.'

Cecil fixed Edward with a steely gaze. 'It is Draycott whose acquaintance I first wish you to cultivate.'

Edward stared back in astonishment. 'He is hardly likely to take kindly to an approach from one of those who he must regard as his enemy — one of those who has been seeking to close down his almost nightly traffic of vagabonds and ne'er-do-wells from Sherwood into the town. We have never met face to face, but he will surely know my name, and of my office as town bailiff.'

'That is why I suggest that you be dismissed from that office,' Cecil replied with a cold smile.

'What?' Edward said. 'I have no doubt that you could bring the necessary pressure to bear on my two sheriffs to part with my services, but I have a wife and three children, with another on the way. What will I do for a livelihood once I've fulfilled whatever fresh duties you have in mind for me?'

'Calm yourself. You will not be dismissed in reality — your employers will simply put it about that you have been,' Cecil assured him. 'And your reference to your wife puts me in mind of something else — do I recall correctly that her parents still reside in a grace-and-favour cottage on the de la Zouch estate, where some years ago you met with a man named Parkin in castle that is under the management of Sir George Hastings, Earl of Huntingdon?'

'You are well informed, sir,' said Edward, 'but what of it?'

'When you are dismissed from office, what could be more natural than for your family to take refuge, and seek alms, from your wife's family, humble though their means may be? And of course you would want to visit the estate on which they live from time to time — where you may pass valuable information to me via the good offices of the earl.'

'I have not agreed to any of this,' Edward protested. 'Pray why should I pretend to be dismissed, and visit my family like an outlaw seeking to hide from the authorities?'

'Because that is precisely what I wish you to become,' Cecil told him. 'A man unjustly dismissed from office, bitter at the treatment afforded him, anxious regarding the welfare of his family, and eager to hit back at those in authority who you blame for your current plight. A man, what is more, who has borne arms in the past and might be persuaded to do so again, if the cause be right.'

Edward's eyes narrowed as the implications of what Cecil was proposing began to sink in. 'In short, a vagrant cast onto the winds of ill-fortune, ripe for recruitment into a rebel army?'

'I could not have expressed it better myself,' said Cecil. 'I want you to start immediately after your notional dismissal, which will be in no more than a day or two. You will go to Sherwood Forest, where you will become yet another of those down on their luck who will be open to suggestions and assistance from Josiah Draycott. I wish you to do so because we believe that the recent incursions into Nottingham organised by Draycott have a deeper purpose, behind which may be discovered the covert hand of Sir Griffin Markham.'

'But what might he be seeking to achieve by flooding the town with vagrants and thieves, apart from the obvious aim of causing trouble for the sheriff and his officers?' Edward demanded.

'Would you wish to take the throne of a nation in so much chaos?' Cecil asked.

Edward was puzzled. 'But if it is only the one town…' he began, then stopped mid-sentence. 'But it *isn't* just the one town, is it?'

Cecil shook his head. 'We have the same reports from several large centres of population, and it would seem to be the result of a determined effort to dissuade James from accepting the Crown. But Nottingham is the only one in which we have a reliable person such as yourself, well placed to get to the centre of the web of confusion and anarchy that is being spun. If we can pin home the source as being Markham, and if we have a man installed within his network, then from him we may move on in order to learn the identities of others who have been drawn into this conspiracy.'

'And with my previous experience with arms I can seem to offer him personal protection, is that it?' Edward asked.

'We believe that you can seem to offer him much more than that, Master Mountsorrel. This band of malcontents is not being assembled merely in order to frustrate the efforts of those commissioned to maintain law and order. It is, we believe, intended to form the basis of a private army. An army, what is more, that will require leaders, generals, those who can instruct others in the art of warfare.'

'And you wish me to present myself as just such a man?'

'Precisely. You will not go unrewarded, and your position as town bailiff will be restored to you once you have fulfilled this vital role in the service of your nation. We do not believe that it will take longer than a month or so for you to get word back to us on the extent of the network, those others who may be part of it, and their state of readiness to stage a rebellion.'

'And should my ruse be detected?' Edward asked. 'May I be allowed to communicate with Francis here, should my true mission be exposed?'

'I was wondering when someone would allocate me a role in all this,' Francis responded grumpily. 'If it is in order to be ready to save Edward's neck from his own foolhardiness, then so be it.'

'You will be well occupied performing duties in both the county *and* the town,' Cecil told him. 'We cannot leave Nottingham without a bailiff for too long, and it would look suspicious if we were to delay replacing the man who has allegedly been dismissed. So the town sheriffs will be advised that you will be undertaking double duties in the short time it will take Mountsorrel to acquire the information we need.'

Francis frowned. 'But what if I am obliged to move against the group that will shortly contain Edward? What then?'

'Then I suggest that you experience a lapse in enthusiasm for the performance of your duties,' Cecil said unpleasantly. 'Do nothing in the vicinity of the forest of Sherwood unless it is necessary to do so in order to rescue your colleague.'

'And how will I know that this is necessary?' Francis objected, but Edward was ahead of him in that.

'The inn at Edwinstowe — the one along the track that heads north towards Swinecote — does it still possess that massive old oak tree in its grounds?' he asked. When Francis nodded, he added, 'Keep it under daily observation, and should you see a red scarf hanging from one of its upper boughs, bring help. It will signify that I am in danger of some sort.'

'But do not maintain regular communication between the two of you,' Cecil insisted, 'since it is vital to our scheme that no-one can associate Edward with the agents of law and order. He is to become an outcast, an "outlaw" like the fabled Robin Hood, and his regular line of communication is to be with the Earl of Huntingdon at Ashby. Are we in *total* agreement with that?'

'We are,' said Edward. Francis remained sullenly silent; whether he was not assured of his friend's safety, or whether he resented the minor role that had been allocated to him, it was impossible to tell.

Satisfied that they had achieved their objective, Cecil and Dalrymple retired for the night, leaving Edward and Francis to walk over to the fruit barn in which Rose and Kitty had made rudimentary sleeping arrangements for them all.

'What do you think will be Elizbeth's likely humour when you advise her that you are once again risking your life for England?' Francis asked.

'What makes you think that I intend to tell her the truth?' Edward replied sadly.

5

With her hands on her hips, Elizabeth left Edward in little doubt of her displeasure.

'I can count on one hand the number of occasions on which you've actually volunteered to take us all down to visit my parents, so you'll forgive me if I entertain the gravest doubts regarding your apparent eagerness to do so on this occasion. What are you up to, Edward?'

'I'm not at liberty to reveal that,' he said, only too aware of the feebleness of his reply. 'It is simply the case that I shall be out of town for some weeks, and it would be better if you and the children were safely installed in the cottage on the Ashby estate, rather than left alone here, at the mercy of those vagabonds and ill-doers who enter the town by night.'

'They've never ventured into this part of the town, so far as I'm aware,' she argued, 'and you clearly have no concerns about leaving poor Meg here on her own, so what's your *real* reason for wanting us all out of the way?'

'I can say no more than I have already,' Edward replied bluntly, 'so do you wish me to accompany you along the uncertain, and possibly dangerous, road south, or will you take that risk upon yourself, bearing in mind that the children will also be at the mercy of any cutpurse, violator or outlaw that you might encounter?'

'Clearly I would be grateful if you could honour your obligations as a husband and father to the meagre extent of ensuring that we reach Ashby unmolested,' she replied coldly, 'but you would do so more convincingly if you revealed the truth behind the need for us to move at such short notice. Why must it be by tomorrow?'

'Again, I cannot give my reasons. If you are apprehensive that Meg may come to harm in the absence of us all, then we may give her leave to lodge with her married sister in Sneinton.'

Elizabeth snorted. 'You imagine that she can simply take herself off there in the hope that she will be welcomed across their threshold? You must at least allow her time to enquire whether or not she will be able to stay, must you not?'

'Of course,' Edward conceded, 'and she may do so this very hour, if it would sweeten your mood.'

Elizabeth strode into the scullery to advise Meg that she had the remainder of the day free, so that she might make arrangements to stay with her sister. Meanwhile, Edward told their excited children that the following day they would be journeying south to stay with their grandparents. Then he took the stairs up to the main bedchamber, seized a calico sack that had travelled with him since his days as a foot soldier, and began to pack what he needed for a few weeks posing as a forest vagrant.

An hour later, he heard a terse conversation taking place in the lower chamber, followed by a shouted command from his wife. 'Come down here and explain yourself — at once!'

Downstairs, a sheepish-looking Meg stood wringing her hands in the doorway that led to the scullery. Elizabeth seemed to loom a few inches taller as she instructed the housemaid, 'Tell him what you just told me!'

Meg looked down at the floor and twisted her hands in the folds of her apron as she croaked out, 'Begging your pardon and all, Master, but it's being spoken all round the market that you've been dismissed from your post.'

'What were you about, diverting from your journey in order to visit the market?' Edward asked in the hope of buying time in which to invent a suitable lie, but Elizabeth was having none of that.

'It's Saturday, you coddle-brain! The swiftest way from here to Sneinton is through the market, even on Market Day. But don't evade the issue — have you been deprived of your office or not?'

'In one sense, yes — but in another...'

That was as far as he got before Elizabeth slammed her hand down onto the table with such force that the salvers left over from breakfast jumped an inch into the air. 'There can only be *one* sense, you turnip head! We are undone, ruined, bereft of the means of survival, doomed to starvation, and you sought to hide that from us by taking us off to visit my parents — no wonder I was suspicious of your motives!'

'If you'd let me explain...'

'Listen to more of your lies, more likely!' she countered angrily. 'Just stand aside while I go upstairs and pack what we will need in order to throw ourselves on the charity of my aged parents.'

'My dismissal is only a ruse!' Edward snapped in desperation.

Elizbeth narrowed her eyes and clenched her jaw. '*Another* ruse, you mean? Like the one that sought to remove us all from the town before word of your disgrace reached us? There was a time when I regarded the day I met Edward Mountsorrel as the answer to all my prayers — I must now assume that I'd been praying to a false god. Out of my way!'

The rest of that day was one of the most miserable that Edward could remember. He gave up trying to explain to Elizabeth that his dismissal was all part of a devious scheme, and instead sought to avoid her by preparing for the family's departure. His horse was fed and rubbed down, his saddle leathers were polished to a shine, his boots were cleaner than they'd been for months, and he even took the time to wash himself from head to foot using water from the butt in the rear yard.

His efforts to avoid his wife were mirrored by her angry packing of the children's clothes, the baking of bread, the salting of fish, and the wrapping of the leftover cheese — tasks that fell to her by default when Meg took herself off with an embarrassed farewell. Elizabeth fed the children at suppertime without advising Edward that there was food on the table, and once the three offspring had been bedded down in the corner of the living chamber, she strolled outside and sat gazing up at the night sky, her face a picture of sad resignation. Some bread and dried fish had been left out on the table, and Edward made himself a frugal meal from that, not that he had any appetite. He then curled up under an old horse blanket next to the children, allowing his wife to occupy the bed upstairs that they would ordinarily have shared.

Edward was saddling the horse and fixing it to the wagon long before the cockerels kept by various neighbours announced the dawn. As he walked back in through the scullery, he saw that Elizabeth had left a mug to the side of the almost empty beer hogshead, so he quenched his thirst as he listened to the happy chattering of the children.

'We're ready,' said Elizabeth coldly. 'You can lead the horse out, if you would be so obliging.'

Edward gloomily lifted the three children into the back of the wagon filled with bags of spare clothing, a bundle of food for the journey, and various other items. Sadly, one of them was Elizabeth's old bible, without which she'd never been known to travel, and which was somehow symbolic of her belief that they would never be returning.

Several silent hours later, they reached the humble cottage that sat to the side of the lodge gates to the Ashby de la Zouch estate. Elizabeth's mother, Catherine Porter, rushed out with a broad smile to welcome her daughter and grandchildren when her husband Edwin announced their arrival from where he'd been sitting outside, whittling a piece of wood into a candle holder.

'Such a wonderful surprise!' Catherine enthused. 'To what do we owe this unexpected blessing?'

'Ask him,' Elizabeth replied sourly with a backward jerk of her thumb to where Edward was lowering little Joanna to the ground as the older children escaped from their grandmother's hugs and ran into the house in search of her gingerbread. Catherine looked uncertainly back at Edward, who shrugged helplessly and began unloading the wagon. His father-in-law Edwin walked back into the house, reappearing several minutes later with a large gourd of homemade beer and two rustic mugs. He waited until Edward had placed the last of their belongings just inside the threshold entrance to the cottage, from which the sound of Elizabeth's strident complaints to her mother were only too audible, then invited Edward to take a seat beside him. 'Slake your thirst after that long ride out of town,' he said.

The question hung awkwardly in the air between them until Edwin spoke again.

'From what our Elizabeth's busy telling her Ma, you must've crossed the wrong folk the wrong way.'

'Far from it, Edwin,' Edward replied, relieved to have found someone who might be prepared to listen to an explanation. 'In fact, I shall shortly be engaged on important business connected directly with my office, and it is only being put about that I've been dismissed, to allow me to fulfil the role that I've been allocated. I cannot say more, due to the oath of secrecy by which I'm bound, but those who've placed their trust in me have instructed that I keep regular contact with the Earl of Huntingdon. Does he still reside in the castle?'

'Yes,' Edwin confirmed, 'and he's improved the old ruin. It don't look a lot like it used to when I were the steward up there, but then life has to move on, don't it? Is it right what Elizabeth was saying — that she's due another child in the summer?'

'Yes, and my reason for bringing them all down here was to keep them safe, which obliges me to disclose a little more of what I shall be about in the next few weeks. Please keep this between us — I only mention it because it may be that I won't be around to see to the welfare of those I love most dearly. I need your assurance that you'll see that they don't starve if the worst comes to the worst.'

'What in God's name have you got yourself involved in?' Edwin asked fearfully.

Edward lowered his voice. 'I can tell you only that what I am embarking upon may reveal a plot against our incoming king, James of Scotland. There are those who would prefer a Catholic monarch, and they are seeking to replace him, possibly by violent means. I am to pretend to be a vagabond sword for hire, and blend in with these traitors, but there is always the risk that they will see through my pretence and that I will pay the price. If that proves to be the case, please promise me that Elizabeth and the children will be well cared for.'

Edwin nodded sagely. 'You surely know you can count on Catherine and me to do that, Edward? They're our family as well as yours, and if owt befalls you, we'll make sure they want for nowt what's within our power to give them. It'll be humble enough, as you can see, but what we can do for them, we will. And Elizabeth, if she did but know it, should be a *very* proud woman, to be wed to such a brave man as yourself.'

'Yes, well, she doesn't stop yelling at me for long enough for me to tell her that,' Edward chuckled as a tear came to his eye. 'But tell no-one what I've just told you, Edwin — not even Elizabeth.'

'From what you were asking earlier, can I take it that the earl up at the castle is involved in all this?' Edwin asked. 'Does that mean you'll be coming back here from time to time, in order to pass messages on?'

'Yes, the Earl of Huntingdon is my means of contacting those from London who've allocated me this dangerous work,' Edward confirmed, 'which must give you some idea of how important my appointed task is to the nation.'

Just then Catherine called that supper was on the table, and Edward made a great show of seating himself between Margaret and Robert, rather than having to make any physical contact with his wife. Meanwhile, Elizabeth busied herself persuading Joanna to eat and ignored her husband. When it came to bedtime, given the cramped accommodation, it was unavoidable that Edward and Elizabeth would have to share the main bedchamber that Edwin and Catherine had given up for them. Edward therefore made a point of taking a turn around the vegetable patch to work off his supper, allowing his wife to prepare herself for bed in private. When he rejoined her, a large spare bolster had been pushed up against her back, and she faced away from him, pretending to be deep in slumber. He sighed, snuggled under the covers, and passed peacefully into a long sleep of his own.

The next morning he awoke to the sound of a busy household preparing breakfast, overlaid with the distant shrieks of the children as they raced around the trees in the modest orchard to the rear of the cottage. He roused himself and walked sleepily into the main room, where the conversation that Elizabeth and her mother had been engaged in ceased abruptly. Catherine made a show of placing fresh bread on the table and unwrapping the breakfast cheese, while Elizabeth gave him a long, curious stare.

'Will you be leaving today?' she asked.

Edward nodded. 'As soon as the sun's fully up. I have a long ride ahead of me.'

'To where?' she asked in a voice that shook slightly.

He looked into her eyes. 'If I told you that I'm sworn to silence regarding that, you'd no doubt accuse me of *more* falsehood, so let me say only that I'll have occasion to take a late supper with Francis, Kitty and Rose.'

Elizabeth left it at that, but ate virtually nothing once the rest of the family gathered round the board and did justice to the hearty spread that Catherine had laid out.

An hour later Edward bid everyone farewell, hugged the children, thanked Catherine and Edwin for their hospitality, promised to return within the week, and walked outside to untie his horse. He had his foot in the stirrup when he looked up and saw Elizabeth standing at the cottage door, her shoulders heaving. He opted to walk the horse towards the door, and as he got closer he saw the tears streaming down his wife's face. He let go of the bridle, knowing that his horse could be trusted not to trot away, and Elizabeth threw herself into his arms with anguished sobs.

'Please, *please* forgive me, Edward!' she choked. 'I've badly misjudged you, but please come back to us — *please*! My father told me everything.'

'How *much* did he tell you?' Edward asked, relieved that he hadn't disclosed more.

'Only that you're about to hazard your life for us, and everyone else in the land. Please don't let us part with angry words, when I may never see you again. *Please*, Edward!'

He placed a hand on each of her shoulders. 'Elizabeth, you're the reason why I remain on this earth. You and our children. Without you, life would have no meaning for me, so don't imagine that I'm about to forego all the happiness of the years that lie ahead. I'm a trained swordsman and an experienced sheriff's bailiff. I'm stronger than most men, and I have the most wonderful woman in the world as my wife. Trust me when I say that I'll be back.'

She clung to him, sobbing piteously and refusing to let go, until Catherine emerged quietly from the doorway and pulled her round so that she was weeping on her mother's shoulder. Edward mouthed his silent thanks, then swung into the saddle and tried to blink away his tears as he headed out towards the track that led north.

'The prodigal returns!' Francis announced as he looked up from weeding between two lines of apples trees and saw Edward trotting in. 'You're too late for dinner, and two hours too early for supper, but come in and have some of Rose's elderflower beer.'

'Francis tells us that you're headed for Sherwood Forest,' Rose announced over the supper table. 'He also tells me to shut up whenever I mention it, so I'll just advise you to take great care in there. By all accounts it's the biggest den of thieves and cut-throats in the county, and even Francis doesn't venture into the forest without a few constables by his side.'

'How did Elizabeth take the news?' Francis asked.

Edward shrugged. 'I didn't tell her the half of it, but at least I think I've persuaded her that my dismissal from office is only a ruse.'

'So when do you set off?' Kitty asked.

'Don't take this as an insult to the comfort of your hearth, but I'll be leaving after the sun rises tomorrow.'

'You should make the outskirts within the first hour,' Francis told him.

Edward shook his head. 'I'll be on foot, if I may leave my horse in your stable. I'm supposed to be a wandering vagrant down on his luck, and I'll be more convincing if I'm not astride a fine stallion. I also plan to wear some old clothes that I brought with me for the same purpose, some of which were in need of a wash when I retrieved them from the pile of cast-offs. I mention that in case any of you were thinking of hugging me goodbye.'

'You flatter yourself,' Francis chuckled.

'I'll say a prayer for your safe delivery from whatever it is you're intending to walk into,' said Rose. 'I can never fully repay my debt to you for saving me from being hanged as a witch.'

'You did that when you restored the spirits of my only son with your magic potion,' Edward assured her, then looked across at Kitty. 'You're very quiet.'

'I just hope that you survive what Francis tells me will be a very hazardous enterprise,' said Kitty. 'For Francis's sake, that is — he won't admit it, but you're like a brother to him.'

'A stupid younger brother,' Francis chimed in to cover his embarrassment.

As the sun began to descend from its full height the following afternoon, with clouds in the west threatening showers, Edward was well north of Edwinstowe. He was heading towards the village of Swinecote along the rutted path that ran through the densest part of Sherwood Forest, in which those he was seeking out had taken to skulking.

He'd kept his sword, but otherwise resembled a vagrant. The smell of old sweat was sour under his armpits, his jerkin was stained with the evidence of many brutal encounters, his boots were beginning to crack in places, and he was walking with a limp after the four-hour tramp north from Daybrook, with only a short rest in Edwinstowe. He had paused here so that word of his passing could travel through the glades from those at the inn who were paid to alert those lurking in the foliage when a traveller was heading their way.

He was just beginning to persuade himself that his long walk had been in vain when there was a loud rustling sound to both the right and left of the track, and into his path moved four burly men, little better dressed than himself.

'That's as far as you go,' said the man who was perhaps their leader. Then he turned both ways to address his accompanying ruffians, armed with crude clubs made from oak branches. 'Mind your manners,' he told them, ''cos it's not every day you get a visit from a bailiff, and not every day you get to string one up by his neck.'

6

'You appear to have the advantage of me,' Edward said. 'You clearly know who I once was, yet your face is not familiar.'

'You probably remember my behind better,' the man growled back, 'since it were that what you kicked afore throwing me into the back of your wagon.'

'You were one of those I removed from the town in my days as a bailiff?'

'Me and plenty more,' the man growled. 'I don't suppose you got round to asking my name then, so let me put you wise. My name's Gedling — Nat Gedling — just so you know who's getting to settle an old score with you.'

'If you did but know it,' Edward said sadly, 'you already did. You and others like you. When I couldn't prevent you invading the town by night, I was dismissed from my office, and now I'm no better served by fortune than you are. In fact, I walked for two days in the hope that I might find a new home here. Or at least something to eat, and perhaps somewhere to lay my head. My house went with my office, you see, and my wife left as soon as I told her that we were ruined. You've obviously all managed to keep body and soul together up here, so perhaps I might.'

'A pretty tale,' Gedling sneered, 'but how do we know that you're not up here just to spy out where we live, then send in soldiers?'

'You don't, do you?' Edward replied. 'But it's the truth that I'm down on my luck. So far down, in fact, that I don't care if you hang me from that tree right now, just like you threatened. I won't even put up a fight, because to tell you the truth, after all that walking, I don't think I've got any fight left in me. So do your worst.'

'I obviously look more stupid than I thought,' Gedling said nastily, then nodded to someone over Edward's shoulder as he commanded, 'Take his sword off him, and tie him up.'

Edward turned. At least a dozen men had crept up on him from behind while he'd been parleying with Gedling, who was clearly their leader. Two of the men walked forward cautiously, then quickened their pace when Edward unbuckled his sword and dropped it on the dusty track with a clatter. Once they had it safely in their possession, they stepped up to Edward and began binding his hands and feet with a crude rope made from intertwined strands of flax. He looked back at Gedling, then nodded towards a tall oak that was overhanging the track.

'That one?' he asked, hoping that it wasn't.

Gedling sneered. 'Not yet, and not that one. We've got a special tree we use for those who cross us. First of all we've got to take you to see the man. They're the rules.'

'What man?' Edward asked.

'You'll find out soon enough. Pick him up and bring him with us, lads.'

Since Edward's lower limbs were tied together he clearly wasn't able to walk, so he suffered the indignity of being tied to two stout poles, then carried, hanging downwards, over the shoulders of four men. It seemed to take forever as they made their way slowly down dark pathways of beaten grass and bracken, deeper and deeper into the increasingly dark foliage. Then they came to a clearing of sorts, and Edward was dumped heavily onto the ground and ordered to sit up, while Gedling ordered someone to fetch 'the man'.

While waiting for him to arrive, Edward was left alone to study — and memorise — his surroundings as the final rays of the afternoon sun flickered in and out between the swaying branches of the canopy of oak, birch and chestnut. There was only one crude structure that could be described as a building, and even that was little better than a series of oak slabs driven into the ground and held together with strong vines. A woman sat outside it in front of a fire, stirring something in the pot that hung over it. Several hungry-looking children sat around her, playing with sticks and stones. The woman looked up at Edward with curiosity, then looked away on a sharp command from Gedling, who was presumably either her husband or the one who gave her orders. Whatever the arrangement, the look of fear in her eyes, and the instinctive flinching away as she doubled over in anticipation of a kick, told its own tale.

As for the rest of the settlement, it consisted largely of rudimentary shelters, some of wood and others of rough canvas sheets, which might keep out a light rain shower but would be useless in a severe storm. The miserable wretches sitting around these shelters appeared to take no interest in Edward, as if the arrival of a man trussed like a hog and hung upside down between two poles was a regular occurrence.

Night had closed in on them. No-one attempted to make Edward more comfortable where he lay trussed up on the damp ground, and no-one offered any food or water. Then he sensed movement and heard a few whispered words of welcome outside the crude shack occupied by Gedling, who then walked towards Edward in the company of another man. It was too dark for Edward to make out anything other than the fact that the newcomer was large, bordering on fat, and that unlike anyone else in this camp he appeared to be well covered, wearing a heavy riding cloak over his doublet and hose. The man stared down at him for a moment before he asked, 'Bailiff Mountsorrel?'

'I used to be,' Edward replied in a tone of resignation.

'So I'm advised, by my people here. My name's Josiah Draycott — presumably you've heard that name?'

'If I did, I've probably forgotten it,' Edward lied, to a responding snort.

'A nice attempt at dissemblance, but I have reason to believe that my name has been revealed to you more than once in your official capacity.'

'My *former* official capacity,' Edward corrected him.

Draycott sighed. 'Word is certainly out that you've been dismissed from your office, and my spies tell me that your dwelling has been abandoned, but how do I know that this is not some devious ploy by the authorities to penetrate our network?'

'In the days when I cared for that sort of thing, it might have occurred to me,' Edward replied with just enough bitterness to sound convincing, 'but the dim-witted oafs who employed me would never have agreed to it, so rest assured. They care too much for sitting on their padded arses and sending bland, reassuring messages down to London that all is well and good regarding their well-rewarded offices. Then, when a representative sent by Secretary Cecil arrived and learned that you and your followers were still entering the town almost unchecked, Sheriffs Littlefare and Hynde, God rot their souls, opted to cast the blame for that onto me, and here I am.'

'Embittered by your treatment at their hands, say you?'

'Wouldn't you be?' Edward retorted hotly. 'But my treatment at the hands of your tribe of ruffians here has been even worse. May I not at least be afforded the freedom of my hands?'

'Perhaps, when we decide what to do with you,' Draycott conceded. 'I am still not assured that you are not here as some sort of elaborate plot, but if you are genuine in what you assert, then it may be that you can be of use to us. You can handle a sword?'

'I could if I had one, but it was taken from me.'

'It may be restored in due course. For the time being, enjoy your first night in our company, and I will give word that you are to be fed in the morning.'

With that he turned and walked back to the dwelling belonging to Gedling. From what Edward could make out of their conversation, he was thanking Gedling's woman for the bowl of rabbit stew that she offered him, and advising her man that he'd be spending the night under what passed for his roof.

Left alone with his thoughts, and with nothing else to distract him, Edward pondered whether or not he'd succeeded in convincing Draycott that he really was down on his luck. The man had proved himself wise enough to make good use of the misfortunes of others, and might find Edward's talents with a sword, and his knowledge of how law and order were organised inside the town, too tempting not to employ them for his own devious purposes. On the other hand, Draycott had survived this long without being brought to account for his actions, and was perhaps not gullible enough to accept Edward's assurances that he was now seeking to become one of his followers.

It was a dark night, although fortunately a dry one so far, and Edward had been left where he'd first been dumped, on a patch of flattened grass on the outer edge of the group of makeshift dwellings. Such sounds as he could hear were consistent with families going about the business of getting fed and preparing to bed down for the night, and the smell of stew was making his stomach growl. If he could get himself free of his bonds, he might be able to steal food from an unguarded pot once everyone was asleep, and the fires were out.

Experience and training had taught him that having one's hands tied, even tightly, behind one's back was no real restraint, and those who'd bound him had been slack in their efforts. He could still move his wrists, and he hadn't lost all sensation in his hands. The first objective was to get his hands in front of him, rather than behind, and this was achieved swiftly via a trick he'd been taught while still a foot soldier in training. He brought his arms under his buttocks, wriggled his legs through the slack loop until his hands were out in front of him, then rested for a few moments in order to regain his breath and reassure himself that no-one was aware of his furtive movements.

It remained silent, apart from the distant rasp of several snores, so Edward used his bound hands to untie the bonds around his feet, then rolled over onto his knees and rose cautiously. He crept towards an area he'd noticed earlier, in which some attempt had been made to grow crops in a cleared patch.

His instincts were rewarded when he located a discarded hoe that still possessed a rusty blade, with which he made short work of the bonds around his wrist, leaving just a few bare threads that maintained the illusion that he was still securely bound. Then he crawled back to where he'd been left and allowed sleep to overtake him.

He was awoken shortly after daybreak by the sound of a woman's screams, almost drowning out the curses of the man calling himself Nat Gedling.

'You'll do as you're told, understand?' Gedling's arm was raised over her bowed head as if about to strike a blow.

'They treat me like a whore!' she was objecting tearfully. 'Last time we were there, two of them took me behind the stables and did what they wanted! I ain't going back there, and there's an end to it!'

'It's all you're fit for, you smelly old goat!' Gedling shouted as he brought his fist down heavily on the side of the woman's head. She fell forward like a heavy rock being heaved into a pond, and in his rage Gedling began kicking her ribs, all but lifting her body off the dirt with every blow that landed.

Edward had seen more than he could stand, and pulled hastily on his bonds in order to free himself. He rose to his feet and raced over to Gedling. 'Stop that at once!' he shouted. 'You'll kill the poor wretch!'

'The "poor wretch" is my woman, and she'll do what I tell her!' Gedling insisted as he continued driving his boot into the woman's torso. 'She was a doxy when I first met her, and she can go back to it if I tell her to. And what's it to you? If it comes to that, how did you get yourself untied?'

'A few tricks of my former trade,' Edward replied as a red mist of anger rose before his eyes. 'Now leave her be, else you'll be answerable to me!'

Gedling gave a shout of scorn as he left off kicking the helpless woman and ducked inside his hovel, re-emerging with the sword that had been confiscated from Edward. 'Now let's see if one of your tricks is how to take on a man armed with a sword!'

He advanced quickly on Edward, waving the sword menacingly at shoulder level, and with a sigh of relief Edward realised that the oaf had never received a single day's sword training, and was about to commit the fundamental error of all beginners. He waited until Gedling began his swing, then sidestepped neatly and brought the full weight of his fist down onto the man's forearm. Gedling dropped the sword with a yell of pain, and Edward grabbed the arm, turned it over, raised his knee and rammed it down hard until he heard the snap of bone, followed by an agonised scream from Gedling as he fell to the ground. Edward gave him one kick in the ribs, just to let him know what it felt like, then looked up as he saw Draycott in the doorway, dressed in his hose and undershirt.

It fell silent as Draycott looked down at the whimpering Gedling and shook his head sadly. Then he looked back up at Edward with a frown.

'It looks as if you'll be joining us after all,' he said. 'Not that you have much of a choice, mind you. It's either that or we hang you — which would you prefer?'

'Will I be fighting or farming?' Edward asked.

'You'll be leading the men in warfare, when the time comes.'

'You mean I've finally convinced you that I just want to stay here and be fed and housed?'

Draycott nodded down at Gedling's writhing form. 'No, I mean that you've just incapacitated the man who was supposed to be training the recruits. Welcome to Sherwood, Master Mountsorrel.'

7

Edward burst out laughing as he looked across at where Gedling was being assisted to his feet, still whimpering and crying out.

'If *that* was the best you had, and his task was to train the other men, then may I congratulate you on a change of fortune? The man clearly had no idea how to use a sword, and he had not the remotest grasp of either common sense or self-defence. Do you have *no-one* here better than that?'

'A few,' Draycott replied, 'but in the main they grow old — veterans of the days when we fought the Armada. Many of them were injured in that endeavour and unable to work for their family's survival. That's why they look to me.'

'You forget that I am of the same vintage,' said Edward.

Draycott merely smiled. 'But you have obviously remained fit and agile, and have remembered what you were trained to do. Most of the older men here were in Her Majesty's navy, and unless I have need of men to command cannon in order to invade by sea, their former skills will be of no use to me.'

'Why do you need an army, anyway?'

'None of your damned business,' Draycott snapped, and Edward realised that he had probably gone too far. This was confirmed when Draycott added, 'Do not believe for one moment that I accept your tale of being down on your luck, seeking merely shelter, comradeship and food. But since you will be remaining in this camp, showing others how to wield a sword, this will give me no immediate cause for concern. In return for your services you will be fed, and you may move into this shack, crude though it is. Gedling will be taken to the house of a bone-setter of my acquaintance, who will repair the damage you have done to him, and then set him to work in his yard. He will not be allowed to return here anyway, after his actions this day.'

'For attacking me, you mean?' Edward asked.

Draycott snorted. 'No, for his stupidity. And, of course, his cowardly brutality towards the woman who has proved so valuable to us with her abilities as a cook. Since you are taking over the man's house, you may also enjoy his former woman, who will no doubt be most generous to you as a reward for saving her neck. And now it is long past the hour when I must set about my business. I shall be returning at sundown in order to lead the next group into the town, and I shall expect to see some sign that you have begun organising the men into some sort of fighting unit.'

'How will I know which men to train?' Edward asked. 'What I mean is, which of them will be journeying into the town?'

'They *earn* that right,' said Draycott. 'If and when they do what they are told for long enough, they get the right to travel to their new lives. So you should have no shortage of volunteers.'

'But what if I train them, then you take the best away into town?' Edward challenged. 'What then of your army?'

'I have answered enough of your questions, which only add to my suspicion that you have been sent to spy on us. When do you expect that the authorities will set about replacing you, if what you allege is true, and you were dismissed? Surely, if there is no replacement appointed almost immediately, it should be easier for my people to enter the town by night in search of their futures? It was only ever you who provided any obstacle to that.'

'I shall take that as a compliment,' Edward replied, 'but in answer to your question, I was ordered to leave matters in an organised and ready state for the county bailiff, Master Barton, to assume double duties. If that arrangement continues, you will find the town even easier to penetrate by night.'

'We occasionally came across this Bailiff Barton during our nightly progress,' said Draycott, 'but he seemed to have little support, with very few men at his command.'

'There is good reason for that,' Edward told him. 'I was, for several years, the bailiff for the county, and my constables were spread far and wide through the outlying villages. And there were few enough of them, so we could never pose any serious threat to a large group of malcontents. I would not imagine that those arrangements have improved.'

'We may make use of your experiences in the county in due course,' said Draycott, 'but for the moment your duties lie here. See to it that you begin to create an acceptable fighting band of men.'

'Do we have any swords?' Edward asked.

Draycott shook his head. 'They will be supplied in due course. How soon will you require them?'

'Not immediately, since men who are learning the rudiments of swordplay pose a great risk to each other if they are let loose with sharp blades before they have mastered their use. In some training bands they wrap the blades with cloth, but the basic manoeuvres can be equally well taught using sticks and tree branches, of which I imagine there is an abundance here.'

'And so I will take my leave,' Draycott said, nodding with approval. 'I shall return ere dusk, bringing a beast for your new woman to cook, so that everyone may be reminded of how much they rely upon me. Yourself included.'

With that he departed, leaving Edward to take a closer look at what he had been invited to occupy for the foreseeable future. From where he was standing, it looked even less inviting inside than he'd imagined. There was a profusion of soiled and crumpled cloth that presumably passed for bedding, and a bench that seemed to have been purloined from an abandoned monastery. Other than that, the miserable hovel appeared to be bereft of any creature comforts, and he transferred his attention to his immediate surroundings as he heard a succession of groans and saw Gedling's abused woman attempting to rise to her feet. Two young children moved listlessly from the dead grey embers of the previous night's fire and attempted to assist, but she waved them away with muttered curses, then fell back on her face with strident cries of pain.

Edward took several steps towards her, then recoiled from her stale and sour stench. Washing facilities obviously did not exist in this particular tinkers' encampment, or if they did she clearly did not make use of them, so Edward took a deep breath and then held out both hands to her.

'Grasp these, mistress, and ease yourself upright,' he instructed her. With many winces and curses that would curdle milk, she rose to her knees, then with further assistance from Edward's strong hands she made it to her feet. The girl who was probably her daughter, and seemed to be no older than Edward's own lass Margaret, brought her a mug containing a brown liquid that smelled as if it had been brewed here in the camp. The woman drank greedily, belched, then looked at Edward with a hint of apology with her eyes.

'I'm in your debt, Master-whoever-you-are,' she said, managing to smile. 'The bastard would've killed me, like he always threatened to do. But you proved to be a match for him, and now he's gone, thanks to you.'

'Is he your husband?' Edward asked politely.

She responded with a bitter laugh. 'In a manner of speaking, I suppose, like every other bastard that I've had the misfortune to fall in with. They treat you worse than their dogs, but they expect you to cook for them, and lay with them when the mood takes them. I'm thinking that maybe you'll treat me a bit better. But go and sit yourself down, and Mary and Jamie can give you something to eat at least.' She looked across at the ragged girl and issued an instruction. 'Mary, give the nice master some of that coney stew I was going to throw in the potage, and bring out the last of the black bread. Then maybe he'd like some of that liquor that the old bastard was always brewing.'

Edward politely refused any of the poison that the woman had been drinking, and only realised how hungry he was when he was presented with some cold stew in an old earthenware pot, along with a large chunk of flat black bread. It was so stale that he had to soften it with his saliva before he could bite into it. But he ate heartily and turned to thank the woman, who had managed to lower herself into a sitting position.

'What's your name?' she asked.

'Edward,' he replied. 'What's yours?'

'I was born Janet,' she replied, 'but round here I go by Janey. The two kids are called Mary and Jamie, and they're both mine, though they have different fathers. That was in the better days, before Robert — that was Jamie's dad — got taken by the sickness. We were left with no option but to take up with Gedling, rotten bastard that he is. But still, we've got you now. I'll look after you proper, I promise, and you'll want for nothing.'

Edward swallowed and sought some way of diverting the conversation. 'That man Draycott said you were a cook — is that right?' he asked.

She nodded, then winced. 'Yes, that's what I'm best at. I'm one of the few women around these parts who was taught how to do that. I do the cooking on that there fire that we'll need to get going again before Master Draycott comes back with that venison he promised. You'll have to help me, if you want to get fed, but I can tell you what to do. First of all, Jamie — go and get some wood to start the fire again.'

The boy ran off as instructed, returning with an armful of kindling. He then raced back and forth several times, carrying more substantial branches and logs to use once they'd got the kindling lit. The fire was coaxed to life in time for the girl Mary to begin mixing grain into a pot of what looked and smelled like curds, proudly claiming that she was about to make bread.

'My cooking skills are what started Gedling giving me that flogging,' Janey told Edward. 'They need a new cook at the big house in Ollerton. Gedling and me sometimes used to go there with Master Draycott, carrying venison to the master. Gedling was keen on me taking the job, but I know that the women servants are treated rough. Last time we were there, two of the men used me badly, and I wasn't about to go back for more. But Draycott thought different, 'cos he was always sucking up to the crowd that lives there, them and their bleeding God. If that's what God's all about, then I want nowt to do with it.'

'So there's a house in Ollerton that Draycott visits, is that what you're telling me?' Edward coaxed her. His curiosity was tweaked, and he saw a valuable source of information opening up.

Janey nodded. 'Yes, full of holy types who pray to their God, then get themselves legless with liquor and take to doing disgusting things with each other, and anyone else who's around.'

'They don't sound much like good Christians,' Edward observed.

Janey shrugged, again wincing in pain from the sudden movement. 'The master himself is, *and* the ones who visit from time to time. It's just the crowd that hangs around the place all the time who do the filthy stuff. But Master Draycott says they pay well, so we're not to upset them by refusing whatever they want.'

'What exactly do they "pay well" *for*?' Edward asked.

'No idea, 'cos we ain't up there very often. In fact, I hope never to go there again.'

'And this big house is in Ollerton, you say?'

'That's right — but why're you so interested in it?'

'Just making sure I stay clear of it, that's all,' he hedged. 'And I'll certainly do my best to prevent you being taken back up there to work as a cook.'

'Bless you!' she whispered.

'I'll help you with the venison later,' said Edward. 'For the moment I'll need to gather all the able-bodied men I can find around the camp and begin showing them how to use a sword.'

'There'll be bread in the middle of the day,' Janey told him, 'so make sure to come back here and fill your stomach.'

An hour later Edward had a dozen men of widely differing ages and states of fitness standing in a line in front of him. He was holding his sword for them to watch as he demonstrated the three basic positions of 'thrust', 'parry' and 'sweep', instructing them to imitate his actions. All his volunteers were holding tree branches, poles or broom handles, and he had no illusion that they were there because they had a burning desire to learn the art of warfare. They were there because they wanted to eat, and had hopes of being among the chosen few taken nightly on Draycott's cart into Nottingham in search of a new life.

As Edward went through the various actions, his mind drifted back to the last time he'd done this, on an estate in Leicestershire to which he'd been sent by Baron Burghley, the father of Robert Cecil who'd recruited him for his current mission. The objective then had been almost identical to the present one, namely to flush out those who were seeking to overthrow a reigning monarch in favour of one more sympathetic to the Catholic cause. The figurehead of the movement had been the same in each case — the enigmatic Arbella Stuart, who resided with her grandmother in the adjoining county of Derbyshire, and who might not even be aware of what was being plotted in her name.

But on the previous occasion there had been a heartwarming bonus for his endeavours, in that he'd been briefly reunited with his mother, who'd been obliged to consign him to a local orphanage because of the circumstances surrounding his birth. The years Edward had spent in that orphanage, under the tight control of another group of Christian brothers, had done nothing to endear him to the faith that they followed. Now he seemed destined to put down one group of them after another.

He tore himself away from his lingering grief over the loss of his mother, who had been killed by a Catholic rebel just a few days after Edward had met her. Instead, he diverted his mounting rage into his present task, thinking about what he had achieved so far. At least he had confirmed that Draycott was the self-appointed leader of a large group of desperate individuals who looked to him for their salvation, and might easily be persuaded to seek it by way of an armed uprising, while in the meantime causing a good deal of chaos and disruption to the authorities. It was now also confirmed that Draycott was in regular communication with a 'big house' in Ollerton that was almost certainly the one described by Cecil, harbouring a man of means who might well be plotting something against the incoming King James.

As described by Janey, there seemed to be a dissolute set of individuals who were associated with the owner of that house, and who could easily be subverted from any loyalty to the Crown if offered the opportunity for endless debauchery. But that was as far as it went, and unless he could somehow contrive to visit this 'big house' or at least find out more about what was going on inside it, he had nothing meaningful to report back to Cecil.

Deep in thought as the sun began to descend, he heard a voice calling to him from the other side of the clearing, and he took his eyes off the men he was drilling. Janey's son Jamie — who could be no older than six or seven, Edward calculated — was waving to him, and seemed to be trying to tell him that he was required back at the shack.

Dismissing the men with the promise that tomorrow they could look forward to a lengthy run through the surrounding forest in order to improve their fitness, Edward walked over to the fire, where a medium-sized deer carcass was lying to one side.

'We've skinned it,' Jamie told him, 'but I need you to help me get it over the fire.'

There was a metal spike lying to the side, and although it seemed strange to be taking instructions from so young a boy, Edward did as requested, ramming the spike clean through the middle of the dead beast. He then helped Jamie to hoist the loaded spike over the naked flames, into which the hot fat from the carcass was soon spitting merrily.

'How long before it's ready to eat?' Edward asked as the first aromas of cooking flesh began to make his stomach gurgle.

Jamie shrugged. 'Depends how often you turn it with that handle on the end, but a few hours anyroad. Mam would know, but she's not feeling well.'

The faint groaning noises from inside the shack seemed to corroborate what Jamie was telling him, so Edward ducked under the lintel, holding his breath against the rank odour of unwashed bodies. He walked to where Janey was lying, moaning with pain and misery while her daughter Mary sat wiping sweat from her brow. The girl looked up and pleaded with Edward to do something for her mother, but all he could offer was sympathy.

It was well into the night before the venison appeared ready to eat, and hungry folk began drifting towards the fire, each of them armed with a knife with which to carve lumps from the cooked beast. The gathering crowd parted to allow Draycott to move to the front, and he nodded towards Edward as he began carving the first slices, as appeared to be his customary right.

'How did you go with the men?' he asked.

Edward smiled reassuringly. 'I've seen worse. Give me a couple of weeks and I'll have them ready to at least *look* formidable, even if I personally wouldn't want to rely on them at my back.'

A loud shriek of pain disturbed the eager feasting, and Draycott nodded towards the hut.

'Is there owt you can do for our cook? We need her fit and well, if we're to keep up the energy of our promised fighting force. And the big house still needs a cook of its own — I was hoping to give them Janey.'

66

At this moment inspiration struck, and Edward realised that there might be a way in which he could organise regular communication with Francis and his household. He faked a look of grave concern as he replied to Draycott's question.

'The injuries inflicted on Janey by that wretch Gedling are serious, and without some sort of learned physic she'll be unavailable as a cook anywhere for some considerable time. But I know of a wisewoman some miles south of here whose charms and potions are so powerful that some have decried her as a witch. She isn't, in my experience, but she's been known to cure even serious wounds after wild alehouse brawls.'

'Can you bring her here?' Draycott asked.

Edward nodded. 'I can if you'd loan me a horse.'

The following morning, after a restless night lying tangled up in dirty bedding and Janey disturbing everyone's sleep with her incessant groaning, Edward climbed into the saddle of the borrowed horse and set off south. Things were beginning to look more hopeful.

8

As Edward trotted the borrowed horse down the rutted lane in Daybrook that led to the orchard estate owned by Francis and his wife, he could see a naked woman standing by the water butt to the side of the apple store and pouring water over her body.

As he got closer, his initial assumption as to her identity proved to be correct, and he could see why Francis had found his wife Kitty so alluring. But she became aware of his approach at the same time, and gave a squawk of embarrassment as she ran into the barn. There was an excited yelp to his right, and out from between the blackberry bushes that lined the path ran a small boy, who gleefully called out, 'Mama's in her nothings!' before scuttling into the house to Edward's left. A few moments later, as Edward was dismounting, the house door opened suddenly and out stalked Francis, sword in hand. He lowered it with a frown when he saw who the visitor was.

'When Richard warned me that a man was spying on my wife's nakedness, I hardly expected it to be the Bailiff of Nottingham. I trust that your arrival bodes more than a desire on your part to view female flesh?'

'Indeed it does, and I am really here to see Rose,' Edward replied with a broad smile.

'She's not so good on the eye as her sister,' Francis replied with a grin.

'And how would *you* know?' asked an aggrieved voice from the doorway, as Rose herself appeared with a skillet in her hand. 'Set about welcoming our visitor, before I wrap this around your knavish head.'

Within an hour they were seated around the large table in the main room that Francis had fashioned for them out of a huge fallen oak, and Rose was laying dish after dish before them. Kitty was still blushing from her early encounter with Edward, and Francis was trying to lighten the mood.

'I bet this is the finest repast you've seen since you left here several days ago. Do you now reside in Sherwood Forest, and does your unexpected return indicate a need on your part to be properly fed? In truth, we haven't dined this well for months, so feel free to return here every week. Sundays would be best — Kitty never bathes on Sundays, in case the churchgoers divert from their journey towards God in order to take in the entrancing view.'

A smart smack across the side of his head indicated Kitty's opinion of his sense of humour. Edward laughed, swallowed the mouthful of pickled pork that he'd been chewing, and brought them all up to date.

'I have thus far achieved even more than I had hoped. I have met with the man Draycott, who is indeed the self-appointed head of a group of vagrants inhabiting a clearing inside Sherwood Forest, while seeking the good offices of a man who owns a big house in Ollerton. I believe that man to be Sir Griffin Markham, to whom Cecil made reference, and Draycott has placed me in charge of training an armed force of sorts. He no doubt intends to offer the army to Markham in furtherance of whatever treasonous plot the man is engaged in. I was given my new duties after I incapacitated his previous champion, and I now appear to occupy a respected position in his rag-tag band. I have also seemingly inherited the woman who goes with my exalted rank of warfare trainer. I think we can put her to good use in our scheme.'

It fell ominously silent as his audience came to uncomfortable conclusions regarding his meaning, and he felt the need to explain further.

'The woman has need of some wise physic as the result of some grievous injuries inflicted on her by her previous man — the one I maimed when he set about her with his boots. That's when I thought of Rose. The woman is seemingly regarded as the camp cook, and Draycott had hopes of offering her services to the Markham house.'

'Where is this leading, Edward?' Francis demanded as he ripped some more chunks from the fresh loaf and loaded it with soft goats' cheese.

'This woman cannot cook in her current parlous state,' Edward went on. 'She is in need of the ministrations of a wisewoman skilled in physic.'

'You came all the way back here to get me to minister to a vagrant rebel?' Rose exclaimed, clearly outraged.

Edward held up his hand in supplication. 'Hear me out — please! I've been trusted by Draycott to come back here and find a wisewoman I assured him that I know, then bring her to the camp in order to heal this woman — her name is Janey. Once I have Rose installed in the camp, my plan is for her to demonstrate her superior cooking skills, so that Draycott persuades her to allow herself to be introduced into the Markham house, from which she can regularly supply me with information. I can then relay that information back here, and Francis can carry it down to Ashby. There he can not only reassure my wife and family that I remain unharmed, but he can also get information down to Cecil in London by way of the Earl of Huntingdon, who now occupies the de la Zouch estate on which Elizabeth is staying with her parents.'

It fell silent until Francis remarked, 'You've obviously done a great deal of thinking on your brief journey back here from Sherwood, but do you think I have nothing better to do than ride regularly into Leicestershire? You forget that I am currently undertaking the bailiff duties for both the county *and* the town.'

'In order that I might seek information regarding what might be a plot against the Crown,' Edward reminded him with a frown. 'You were present when Cecil decreed that whatever I discover should be relayed through the Earl of Huntingdon. If I am to fulfil my appointed role in all this *and* maintain the pretence that I am a landless wandering vagrant, then I can hardly request leave to visit my wife and family comfortably ensconced in the tranquillity of a Leicestershire estate. Can you think of any better way of achieving our objective?'

While Francis was thinking up a suitable response, Rose let out a sound of exasperation.

'Did anyone deem it appropriate to ask for my opinion?' she asked. 'Edward, I do not pretend to understand what lies behind all this skulduggery, but it seems that you are asking me to use my skills as a wisewoman and a cook to help you gain access to some suspicious house. Given the fact that if it were not for you, I would almost certainly have been hanged as a witch some five years past, I do not regard your request as onerous. I would welcome the opportunity to employ my healing skills in something other than assuaging my sister's morning vomiting and occasional back pains. As for cooking, well, it will be a nice change to be preparing meals for dozens, rather than three people who, although I love them dearly, can on occasions be far too fastidious in their tastes.'

'Thank you, Rose,' Edward beamed with a triumphant glance at Francis. 'What will you need to take with you?'

'That will depend entirely on what ailments I am required to cure,' Rose replied. 'Tell me all you can regarding this woman's condition.'

'She was kicked heavily in the ribs by a brute of a man wearing heavy boots,' Edward told her, 'and thereafter she has complained of pains with every movement of her body. These pains prevent her from sleeping, hoisting meat onto a spit and preparing grain for breadmaking. There are days on which she complains that even breathing causes her discomfort, and she has been like this now for several days, with no sign of any improvement.'

Rose nodded sagely. 'Henbane and willow bark will take away most of the suffering, but her chest must be tightly bound for the time being, which will further restrict her movements.'

'Thereby justifying your assumption of the cooking duties,' Edward pointed out eagerly. 'This is proceeding in a most encouraging fashion!'

'That will depend upon how well I can cook under primitive conditions,' Rose replied. 'Is there a fire burning at all times, and have they established some sort of rudimentary oven?'

'A fire, certainly,' Edward replied, 'but it is an open one, and is allowed to go out at night.'

Rose sat deep in thought for a moment, then looked up and nodded. 'I can take some old iron pieces that were given to us when we acquired the land on which to expand our orchard some three years ago. In the main they are old ploughshares, but they will serve as griddle plates, and if you can undertake to keep the fire stoked around the clock, then we can soon establish enough heat to ensure the adequate cooking of roasts. Do you have a supply of water close by?'

'I believe that there is a stream to one side of us,' said Edward, 'since I regularly see pitchers of water being brought into the camp. But I cannot vouch for its quality.'

'That's of no concern,' said Rose knowingly, 'since a piece of cheesecloth will filter out any impurities. But I shall need to take the wagon, in order to carry all those things I shall need. Will your borrowed horse be fit to haul it?'

'If not, then I'll take mine, assuming that it still resides in your stables,' said Edward. 'But let us begin loading now, in order to set off at first light tomorrow.'

'I hope you know what you're about,' Francis mumbled to Edward as they stood to the side later that afternoon, watching Rose putting bag after bag of undisclosed items over the side into her small wagon. 'Kitty will be bereft should anything ill befall her sister.'

'I'll guard her life with mine,' Edward promised, 'and I'm sorry to have burdened you with further duties. How are matters in town these days?'

'Suspiciously quiet,' Francis replied. 'Even the nightly brawls seem to have diminished in number, and so far as I can tell there have been no further inroads into its northern parts from vagrants from Sherwood.'

Edward nodded. 'I was certainly not aware of any large departures from the camp, but I was intending to speak with you about that. In the main you guard the road south from Mansfield, do you not? The one that passes here?'

'That and the North Road that comes down directly from Sherwood, the one you must have taken to get back here,' Francis replied. 'We set up our traps just north of Arnold, in the woods that adjoin the track at Redhill. Why?'

'Why do you think?' Edward said with a look of great satisfaction. 'I intend to impress Master Draycott by leading his next mission of misery clean into town unmolested, making use of my familiarity with the track down through Bestwood, and from there by way of Bramcote, Chilwell and Beeston villages into the west of the town. I will need you to remain on guard at Redhill, in order that we may pass unseen to the west of you.'

'Will that not require you to pass through Chapel Bar?' asked Francis.

'You forget my frequent journeys out to Wollaton over the years, both when I was playing suit to Elizabeth under her master Willoughby's nose, and when he was sheriff of the county for a year. There is a narrow lane that takes the traveller by way of the former priory at Lenton into the north of the town at Backside.'

The sun was just announcing its arrival over Mapperley Ridge to the east the following morning as Rose bid farewell to Kitty. Francis grasped Edward's hand as he wished him good fortune and pleaded with him to guard his safety, along with that of his travelling companion.

Edward then leapt onto the front board of the wagon and flicked the reins. The old nag pulled forward with many creaks and rattles from the load behind it. As they turned right into the road that would take them, by way of Arnold and Edwinstowe, into the heart of the forest occupied by the outlaws, Rose had one remaining question.

'This woman who I am to treat — have I your assurance that there is nothing carnal between the two of you?'

'You have my assurance,' said Edward, chuckling. 'And you will be even more convinced when you meet her.'

'It hurts like hell!' Janey protested as Rose tightened the binding cloth and nodded for Edward to pin the layers together.

'The pain will slowly subside, provided that you take this simple three times each day,' Rose assured her, handing over the henbane and willow bark that she'd mixed with some elderberry wine.

Janey scowled, knocked it back in one gulp, shuddered, then said, 'If you say so. But did I hear right about you making the dinner?'

'Of course,' Rose assured her. 'But you all look half starved, and it will be some hours before we get that beast cooked fit to eat, so in the meantime I'll make us all some bannocks with the oats I brought with me. All I'll need is some water, if your young son would oblige me?'

Jamie took off at once, and after mixing her oats in enough water to make the mixture sticky to the touch, Rose poured it onto the hot griddle that Edward had placed over the roaring fire he'd lit. Each portion landed on the converted ploughshare with a reassuring sizzle. The supply seemed endless, and within the hour the entire family were gleefully consuming hot bannocks. Word soon spread, and after two more hours there were no more oats left, but over thirty residents of the forest encampment were thanking Rose profusely for her kindness, and praising her skill. She turned her face away from the small crowd that was still gathered around the fire, and whispered in Edward's ear. 'They think *that* was a miracle? Dig me a large hole in the ground and I'll soon become a saint in their eyes.'

By the time the sun had begun to descend from its full height, Edward and Jamie had dug a large hole out of the flinty ground. Meanwhile, Janey had been seated carefully on the bench outside the crude wooden dwelling, supervising her daughter Mary as she skinned a large sheep that some of the men from the camp had captured and slaughtered the previous day. A curious crowd gathered as Rose instructed Edward to place a second old ploughshare that she'd brought with her into the bottom of the hole, then light a fire under it. Once the fire had begun to burn merrily, she supervised the placing of a third lump of spare metal on top of the first, then sent Jamie in search of several sturdy tree branches with which the top metal plate could be levered to one side once it was glowing red from the heat.

A larger crowd of bemused spectators had gathered by the time the top plate was pulled to one side for long enough for the sheep carcass to be placed on the lower plate, then covered with the upper plate once the fire had been stoked back into a glowing mass. Then to everyone's amazement Rose instructed Edward and several of the men standing around the pit to cover the entire assembly back over with the earth that had been first removed in order to create the hole.

'Now what?' Edward asked as his bewilderment got the better of him.

'Now we wait,' Rose said with a smile. 'And while we do so, pray advise me where I'll be lodging once the sun goes down.'

In truth Edward had not given a single thought to that obvious domestic arrangement, and with a good deal of embarrassment he offered Rose his place in the crude wooden dwelling behind them. 'It is somewhat malodorous, as you will have occasion to note,' he said apologetically.

'Typical town man,' said Rose. 'I imagine that you have never slept alongside cattle and pigs in order to keep warm on a winter's night?'

'No, only my horse,' he admitted, 'but if you are content…'

'I will be when I know where you will be sleeping, if you give up your place inside yon palace of pestilence.'

'On the ground, by the remains of that fire you had me create in the hole,' he told her. 'The earth above it will retain its warmth for at least a day, I calculate. Let us hope that the sheep carcass you buried in there does not taste of earth when it is brought back up among us.'

That occurred long after the sun had dipped below the treeline to the west, and six men between them prodded and poked the earth until the top metal cover had been removed, and a glowing roast assailed their hungry noses. They were obliged to wait until the lamb had cooled sufficiently to allow slices to be cut from it by eager camp residents armed with knives. Edward ensured that an orderly line was formed by the men so they could take turns carving enough to feed their families.

The crowd were soon singing Rose's praises and calling down God's blessing upon her. There was still half a roast left when they parted to reveal the arrival of Josiah Draycott.

'Is what I am being advised true? Did your wisewoman dig a hole in the ground, therein to cook a sheep for the entire company?' he asked as he gazed around in amazement and took out his knife to sample the communal roast.

Edward nodded towards Rose. 'She did indeed, and allow me to present to you my old friend Rose Middleham.'

'A cook as well as a wisewoman?'

'No-one surpasses her in either skill, Master Draycott. It is a pity that she never married, in order to pass on her knowledge to any offspring.'

'So there is no family awaiting your return?' Draycott asked, addressing Rose.

'A sister only,' she replied, 'but she is married with a family of her own.'

'How would you like to be engaged in a big house, preparing meals for a gentleman of quality and making such use of your talents with physic as he may require?'

Rose smiled modestly. 'It would not be for the first time, good sir.'

Draycott grinned, revealing the absence of several front teeth, then looked up at Edward. 'Tomorrow this lady and I shall journey to Ollerton. You shall provide our escort.'

'I fear that it went almost *too* well,' Edward confided as he and Rose sat before the embers of the fire, once everyone else had retired to their various sleeping places.

Rose placed a hand on his arm. 'It was what you set out to achieve, was it not? A good man such as yourself should not fear failure when God is on his side.'

'I hope that your satisfaction with how matters have played out is in no way diminished when you have to crawl into that wooden hellhole behind us.'

'I intend to do no such thing,' said Rose as she snuggled closer to him. 'Open your arms and lie chastely with this old lady while you keep her warm through the night.'

9

A line of Judas trees stood sentinel on either side of the long approach to Ollerton Hall, resplendent in their pink foliage. Draycott led the way along it, Edward and Rose following behind on Rose's cart, with Edward's borrowed horse hitched to its rear panel. The drive widened as it opened out onto a flat expanse of freshly scythed grass on which a group of young men were intent on their game of bowls. This denoted them as gentry, since the late queen had banned the playing of it by 'lesser sorts', and the intensity of their curses as a long sweeping pass failed to reach its mark suggested that large sums of money had been wagered on the outcome of the game.

They trotted slowly past the assembled company as Draycott, who knew the layout of the grand estate, led them up the left-hand side of the ornate building towards what Edward assumed would prove to be the scullery door. Before they reached the side path he took the trouble to familiarise himself with the general appearance of the grand dwelling as it glowed a deep red in the morning sun.

It was typical of those recently erected residences with which the gentry sought to impress each other, and attract royalty as house guests. Its lower courses, to a height of at least fifteen feet, were constructed from red brick. The overall layout of the impressive dwelling was in the shape of a giant letter 'E', with what looked like the main entrance recessed into an open courtyard. In front of an ornately carved set of double doors sat a coach with an open door, a footman in attendance in case his master should choose to step out on a whim. Each arm of the E shape was fronted by double bay windows of heavily mullioned glass, above each of which was a heavy stone drip mould into which had been carved images of fantastic beasts. The bay windows in the east wing had been graced with stained glass in the manner of a cathedral, and even from a distance Edward could make out the multi-coloured robes of saints and the gold of seraphim floating around their heads. The glass had almost certainly been purloined from an abandoned holy house in the days when they had been shut down by the late queen's father. The overall effect was as if someone had added a place of worship to a substantial country residence. A forest of ornately carved brick chimneys set into the roofline gave promise of roaring fires in the many rooms of the dwelling. Whoever had ordered the construction of Ollerton Hall had clearly not been wanting for wealth.

Draycott led the way through a scullery in which several women were sweating as they scoured serving dishes to a fresh shine in pans of steaming hot water, and then through an arched opening into the largest kitchen Edward had ever encountered, eliciting sounds of admiration from Rose. There were several flames blazing in recessed open fireplaces, and given that the dinner hour was not far away they each had a spit iron on which a sheep, pig or cow was being turned by a red-faced spit boy seated on a stool. On the tables to the centre of the massive room were large metal pans in which sat pies, pastries and loaves of bread that were being dusted with chopped coriander, or glazed with honey, depending upon their contents. The noise was incessant, as those who appeared to be in charge yelled orders. A small group of liveried servers stood resignedly to one side, awaiting the moment when the first-course platters would be entrusted to them for their short journey up the service stairs into the main hall.

They stood silently for a few moments, surrounded by the noise and steamy heat, until a huge woman in a heavily stained apron waddled up to them, and was about to order them back outside when Draycott managed to convince her that they were here in order to meet with 'the master'. She nodded, then made her way through an archway on the other side of the kitchen, reappearing a few moments later with a rotund, middle-aged man who beckoned them across the kitchen in order to join him on its far side, under the archway.

'It's Master Draycott, as I recall?' the man asked. When Draycott nodded in confirmation, the man led the way down a dingy stone passageway that led further into the house.

'That's the steward, Ralph Condor,' Draycott muttered for Edward's benefit, just as they reached a small parlour into which the man invited them with a wave of his hand. Once they were all standing in the narrow confines of a room with heavily panelled walls but little furniture, he addressed them.

'What business brings you to meet with my master?' he asked.

'I have the pleasure to be presenting, to your master and my very generous benefactor, not only a new cook for his kitchens, but also a man to lead the armed force he hopes to offer to the new monarch,' said Draycott.

'Thank the good Lord for the former,' Condor said with a grimace. 'The woman who currently enjoys that title is drunk from dawn until dusk, and it is a miracle that we have not all been poisoned. Were it not for Lily and Mary, who watch every action she takes, the kitchen would long ago have gone up in flames. As for the unfortunate scullion boys, they are raw from her constant beatings when the strong liquor has her in its thrall.'

Rose kept tactfully silent, and Condor nodded towards Edward.

'As for him, he will need a miracle of his own to create a force of fighting men out of the idle blowhards who hang around the master, fit only for service in the stews or cockpits of the town. They loudly claim that one day they will be possessed of much gold, but all that they have to their name are their idle boasts, fuelled by the master's forbearance and generosity.'

'I will be bringing my own men, trained by me,' Edward told him.

'You will if the master permits,' Condor replied dismissively. 'But you will all wait a while to speak with him, since the service of dinner is about to commence, and the master is as devoted to his stomach as he is to God.'

'Should we depart and return later?' Draycott asked.

Condor shook his head. 'Given the rapidity with which the master consumes his meals, it should want little more than an hour or so. Have you yourselves perchance eaten before coming here? I see the sad shakes of your heads, so follow me to the servants' hall, where you may quell your hunger. On most days the food is fit to be eaten, mainly because it was on the master's supper table the evening before. Come with me.'

A short while later Rose was examining a piece of venison that was impaled on her eating knife and shaking her head in warning to her companions.

'Deny yourselves the roast, if you wish to live to see tomorrow's dawn. This meat is nowhere near cooked enough to kill the disease that it almost certainly carried within it when abandoned in the kitchen by some knave of a butcher. The fruit does not look too bruised, the bread is only from yesterday to judge by its resistance to the touch, and the cheese is sour milk at best, and will do you no harm, if eaten sparingly. As for that which claims to be beer, my donkey's piss has more body in it than that.'

Fully warned, both of her male companions picked listlessly at stale manchet. At length Steward Condor reappeared and announced, 'The master wishes me to admit you now, if you have dined enough.'

'Enough to make my gut gripe,' Edward muttered as they left the servants' hall by way of the staircase that led back up to ground level. Once back in the natural light, they saw that it was approaching the middle of the afternoon, and were relieved that an overnight stay would not prove necessary. Condor knocked confidently on a heavily studded oak door on the far side of the entrance hall, then entered the chamber beyond. He reappeared a moment later and held the door wide open.

'Pray enter and state your business with the master,' he said as he stood to one side to allow them to pass into the hall. It was a massive chamber of a proportion that would, in previous generations, have accommodated an entire royal retinue, from the highest nobles in the land to the meanest cleric in holy orders fulfilling the role of royal chaplain. A huge log fire burned in an ornate fireplace, and the long table down the centre of the hall would, in a former age, have seated at least sixty armed men, all with their squires in attendance. But since this was not a former age, it was easy to conclude that Sir Griffin Markham was a vain man as well as a wealthy one, and that whatever had caused him to be banished from the court of the ageing Queen Elizabeth some ten years ago had almost certainly involved a vainglorious pride.

Markham looked up from fondling one of the two wolfhounds that sat on the rich carpet surrounding the table.

'My steward tells me that you bring me a cook at long last,' he remarked as he gave Rose an appraising glance, 'but from memory she is not the one you offered me before, who proved so popular with several of my guests here in Ollerton.'

'She met with an unfortunate accident,' Draycott wheedled, 'but the one I bring you in her stead is also a wisewoman skilled in the use of simples to cure all manner of maladies.'

'To cure the consequences of her own cooking, you mean?' Markham joked, and everyone smiled except Rose. Then Markham nodded towards Edward. 'Who is he — your manservant?'

'Indeed not,' said Draycott, puffing proudly. 'He's my new men at arms trainer.'

'What became of the previous one — that gruff oaf whose woman was to have been our new cook?'

'He was maimed — by *this* one,' Draycott explained, 'which is why I recruited him to train the armed band that you have been seeking.'

The look that Markham gave Draycott left no-one in any doubt that he'd said the wrong thing, and Edward made a mental note that for whatever purpose an 'armed band' was required by Markham, it was not something he wished to have spread abroad. To cover his embarrassment, Draycott persevered in his attempt to impress his patron.

'This man is Edward Mountsorrel, and until recently he was bailiff to the Sheriff of Nottingham, and one of the greatest obstacles to my efforts to enable Sherwood people to move into the town.'

'And yet you have recruited him into your service?' Markham demanded, his eyebrows raised. 'Have you lost your wits, man?'

'No — I lost my office,' Edward chimed in. 'Master Draycott may consider that I was a thorn in his side when seeking to impose vagrants on the town, but my employer the sheriff thought otherwise, and I was dismissed. I no longer have the use of a house in the town, I have no continuing stipend with which to provide for my family, and my wife has taken our children into a neighbouring county, there to rely on the charity of her aged parents.'

'So you are bitter against authority?' Markham asked, to which Edward replied with a sneer and a muted curse. Markham nodded in Draycott's direction. 'So now that he has turned, your nightly passage into the town will be much less hazardous?' he asked.

'Yes, and he has enough experience to train men to fight,' Draycott replied eagerly. 'He has already begun to do so at our camp.'

'Those who are trained in warfare will not be transferred into the town, surely?' said Markham. 'They must be ready to march to London in the service of — of the new monarch, under my ultimate command, with this man at their head, perhaps. How many may we expect?'

'Twenty or so, to judge by the numbers who have so far stepped forward,' Edward answered. 'But on our way here I espied a fine body of young men on your lawn, engaging in a game of bowls when they might perhaps be added to my trained band.'

Markham looked horrified and shook his head vigorously. 'They are all my guests, and are far too high born to soil their hands in exchanges of arms.'

'They would not be the first nobles to do so,' Edward reminded him. 'Some of our finest military leaders have been drawn from the very highest levels of society. I myself served under the Earl of Leicester in the year in which Spain attempted to invade.'

'Were you in the land force that defended Devon?'

'No, at Tilbury, defending London in case the Spaniards succeeded in defeating the fleet under Effingham,' Edward replied proudly.

Markham nodded. 'The reason why I enquired is that the man who rallied the land forces in Devon was, at that time, its vice-admiral, and highly regarded by our late queen. He is now the Governor of Jersey, and I thought that you might have made his acquaintance. His name is Sir Walter Raleigh.'

'The name is familiar to me, although I know not how,' Edward replied. 'But he is surely another example of those I alluded to earlier — high born, but not reluctant to take up arms.'

'Raleigh no longer bears arms for the nation's defence,' Markham told him, 'and I mention him only in connection with our earlier discourse. He is the reason why those fine young men taking their ease on my lawns are staying here temporarily. They are on their way to join him at Plymouth. Raleigh is an experienced mariner, and on his many voyages he has learned of the existence, somewhere in the Americas, of a city built from pure gold. It is called El Dorado, and Sir Walter is determined to discover it and dismantle its buildings to transport them back here to England. This will require a band of men eager to bend their bodies to heavy labour in return for rich reward — the very men you saw on my lawns. You can now see why they might regard the mere swinging of swords and cutting off of limbs as a poor alternative.'

'Indeed,' Edward conceded as his mind raced with possibilities, 'but might I perhaps request the use of those lawns for the exercise and training of my men? The clearing we have in Sherwood Forest is too hemmed in by trees to be of any value when teaching men how to charge in formation, whereas your open grass would be ideal.'

Markham frowned. 'From what I have myself experienced — as a cavalryman under Essex during the recent Irish Wars — that would have the effect of churning up the grass beyond recall, and my bowling green is the talk of the county. However, there is land closer to the road — rough pasture that is used for cattle in winter, when the snows set in. You may make temporary use of that, should it serve your purpose.'

It did indeed serve Edward's purpose, since it gave him an excuse to revisit Rose once she was installed in the kitchens, and keeping her eyes and ears open to what might be happening on the Markham estate. He smiled and offered a brief word of thanks.

'We have some urgent business that we must address privily, Draycott,' Markham announced. 'Perhaps our new cook might be granted immediate access to the kitchens, there to take up her new duties?'

Without waiting for any formal consent to this suggestion, Markham called for Steward Ralph Condor, who led Edward and Rose back down the service stairs. Once they were back in the confines of the main kitchen, he advised those who were seated on the dirt floor or lying across benches that they had a new cook.

'And what's to happen to *me*, then?' demanded the lady who was being replaced, raising her bloated red face from the bench over which she'd been draped.

Condor grimaced. 'You can go back to poisoning your sister's family in Newark, assuming that you can make it back that far. Your opportunities to make us all ill have just expired, so be on your way.'

There was mild cheering, and a few ruder noises, as the outgoing cook pushed herself to her feet and wobbled uncertainly towards the door.

Rose smiled at the remaining company. 'Things will be different around here from now on. Which of you are called Lily and Mary?'

Two women raised their hands uncertainly from where they sat on the floor, resting their backs against the wall.

'I hear good reports of your work, so you shall be my closest assistants. The first task for us all will be to restore this kitchen to a state of cleanliness, which we may begin just as soon as I have had the opportunity to place my belongings in my new lodging. Perhaps Master Condor would be so good as to show me where that might be found?'

The steward took Rose and Edward out to the courtyard, and indicated a narrow window immediately above the door to the stables. 'You go up that staircase at the side of the tack room inside the stable, but you will need to wait until it has been emptied of its previous occupant. I'll detail two of the grooms to achieve that, and in the meantime you might wish to lift your belongings from the cart that brought you here.'

This gave Edward and Rose the perfect excuse to huddle together out of earshot, as Edward made a great show of lifting down Rose's travel bags.

'Well, I'm here,' said Rose proudly. 'I am required merely to keep my eyes and ears open to whatever I can learn regarding what goes on in this place — is that not so?'

'It is indeed, Rose, and thank you most heartily for being so accommodating,' Edward replied as he leaned down and kissed her cheek. 'You heard me make an excuse for returning here regularly, when we can contrive to meet in order that you may pass on what you have learned. Should we need to take you back to Daybrook, simply let it be known that you wish to visit your sister, who is with child and in need of physic, and that you require my services to guard your person as you journey back south. And so I wish you God's blessings, along with renewed thanks for your courage.'

At that moment Draycott appeared around the corner of the main building and called out to the head groom for their horses to be brought out. They saddled up and began to trot their mounts down the main drive, Draycott glancing behind him with a frown of annoyance.

'A pity that we had to leave that wagon behind, since we could have made use of it this night.'

Edward looked at the sky. 'It wants an hour to sunset yet. What had you in mind?'

'It is time that we introduced more of our number into Nottingham,' Draycott replied. 'We are becoming more numerous by the day, which means more mouths to feed, and we have no cook worthy of that name.'

'I hope you will not take any of my intended fighting men,' Edward replied.

Draycott looked across at him with a knowing smile. 'That will be a matter for you, Edward, since you will be leading them.'

'I thought that this was a task you retained for yourself.'

'Indeed it is, and I did not say that I would not be with you. But it shall be your task to lead the party into the town in which you are no longer welcome and have no remaining authority. Let us see how well you acquit yourself when your successor seeks to oppose us.'

10

There was no moon, and the constant rain showers that had persisted into the second week of May had made the track muddy in places. The atmosphere was oppressive, the night air was sticky, and there was a discontented muttering audible from within the moderately sized group that Edward was escorting down the track between the high hedgerows south of Strelley Village.

'You would not suppose that I am guiding them to a new life,' Draycott complained to Edward, riding alongside him at the head of the several wagons to their rear. 'There's no gratitude to be had from some folk.'

'In the main they are old men,' Edward reminded him. 'Riding a wagon along a rutted lane sets off an aching in their bones, and they are feeling the clammy heat of a sultry night in early summer. They also have no more idea of what awaits them than we do. In my last few weeks of office, we were achieving considerable success in rounding up your "foreigners", as we called them, and sending them back to you.'

'We only selected old men because you insisted on keeping the younger ones to train as soldiers,' Draycott retorted.

Edward was in no mood to be bested in an argument. 'And I'm only attempting to train soldiers because you demanded it of me,' he replied tartly, 'and I'm compelled to observe that they're a sorry bunch.'

'I only hope that you haven't alerted any of your former colleagues to our progress south,' Draycott muttered. 'And where in God's name have you led us, anyway? Our previous approaches have always taken us by way of Arnold.'

'Which is the very reason why you were frequently headed off before even reaching the town,' Edward pointed out. 'Your route was too predictable, which is why we are taking a track well to the west of your previous journeys. And had I a mind to betray you, we would have been challenged long before now. That last village we passed was called Strelley, and within the hour, if fortune smiles upon us, we should be approaching the hills that protect Bramcote from the elements. From there we may either head further south into Chilwell and Beeston, and by that route approach Lenton from the west, or we can take a shorter route via the Wollaton estate of the Willoughby family, which in turn leads to Lenton via a merchant track. Either way you will enter Nottingham without arousing any interest, and my task will have been accomplished.'

'You intend to hang back once we reach Lenton?'

'Once I've shown you the track that will take you to the start of the thoroughfare they call "Backside", certainly,' Edward insisted. 'My face is too well known in the town.'

'Why do I suspect a trap?' Draycott challenged him.

'Because of the life you lead. A life full of intrigue, dishonest dealing, underhand behaviour and betrayal. You exploit the weakness of others and turn it to profit. Little wonder that you suspect a knife in your back at every turn, living such a life.'

'A life you have chosen to join.'

'I had little choice,' Edward countered, 'but I suspect that you did.'

'You intrigue me,' said Draycott as they took the track back north an hour later, having given their party their last instructions. The party they had led out of Sherwood had been told by Edward to follow the track that was clearly marked by the wheel ruts of generations as it wound its way from the ruins of the now abandoned Lenton Priory towards the north-western outskirts of Nottingham. Draycott had added that once in Backside they should repair to The Partridge, and there announce their arrival to one Nathaniel Brewer, names of which Edward made a careful mental note.

'Why should I intrigue you?' Edward challenged him. 'Because I am an honest man beset by bad fortune?'

'Partly that, and partly the impression you convey that you cannot be corrupted out of beliefs and principles that you hold dear. Does that come from your faith?'

'My faith in myself, certainly,' Edward replied. 'As for any Christian faith, those who have professed it to me in the past have proven themselves to be little better than blackguards and mountebanks, peddling false beliefs along with trinkets that are intended to trick the poor and credulous out of their precious pennies.'

'So you have been exposed to the Church?'

'In a sense, yes. I was abandoned as an orphaned baby by a mother who had been got with child by a man professing to be a priest while flaunting the vow of chastity. I was committed to a poorhouse run by so-called holy brothers who were guilty of all the other sins, most notably gluttony, while we were left near starving. I escaped from there to work on the estate of a family that hid their priests from Her Majesty. I was then enlisted as a man at arms to stand against the most powerful Catholic ruler in the world, Philip of Spain, whose torturers were known among gaolers throughout the world. Then I served a queen whose spies listened to men's true devotions through keyholes, and condemned their priests to death, all in the name of the proclaimed "new religion". A pox on *all* religions, Master Draycott, and now let us speak of something more amenable to my humour.'

'Very well. I wish you to have a full company of competent soldiers ready within a month,' said Draycott bluntly.

'There is barely a man among them who is even physically fit, let alone ready to use a sword in the manner for which it is designed. And might I be allowed to know why such an urgency has overtaken your immediate ambitions, whatever they may be?'

'You may not,' Draycott replied sharply. 'You need only know that when the new king is crowned, it is the wish of Sir Griffin Markham that he be in a position to take a worthy company of eager subjects south in order to demonstrate his loyalty to the new order.'

'So it matters not whether the men can fight — simply that they *look* as if they can, am I correct?' Edward asked in disbelief.

'You have the matter correctly summarised. Now where exactly are we, and how soon may we expect to regain the safety of Sherwood?'

Rose had lost no time in making her presence felt in the kitchens of Ollerton Hall. On her first full day she'd ordered everyone to set about scrubbing surfaces clean, ridding the floor, fireplaces and working tables of all the grime that the previous cook had allowed to accumulate. She made a point of befriending the two women, Lily and Mary, who'd first impressed her with their apparent enthusiasm for the various operations involved in serving three meals a day to a large and varied household. Through her conversations with them, she had quickly grasped the essential matters that would require her attention.

She was told by Lily, the older of her two confidantes, that there had been a third woman, Annie, working alongside them until recently. She'd been dismissed when it became known that she was with child, and the master had disapproved of such blatant immorality within what he regarded as a household upholding the highest Christian values.

'A pity he doesn't insist that the young coxcombs around the place abide by the same rules,' Lily complained as they sat by the scullery door, enjoying the fresh air and warm early summer sun. 'They're just ne'er-do-well fools with high opinions of themselves. If it's all the same to you, Mistress, I'd be obliged if you'd not send me where they take their meals, although I'm hopefully a bit too old for them to be taking liberties with, like they did with Annie.'

Rose felt chilled as she took in the implications of what she'd just been told. 'So the group of young men who seem to be living here have their meals served to them in a separate place?' she asked.

Lily shuddered as she nodded. 'Yes, over in the west wing there, where they live, sleep, eat and do all else. They drink, mainly — you wouldn't believe what a midden those lubberworts have made of the chambers they were given by the master in his kindness and generosity. They're in their cups well before the sun's set every day, and when the food's served for supper, God help any serving lass they take a passing fancy to. Like poor Annie — she can't rightly claim any atonement for her condition, because there was more than one of them, and more than one time.'

'Let me see if I understand what you're telling me,' Rose responded once the horror sank in. 'Annie went in there to serve their meals, and they — they — well, they "took advantage of her", as the saying goes. Is that right?'

'Depends how you regard "taking advantage", as you call it,' Lily muttered. 'She weren't willing, let's put it *that* way. But there was a few of them, by all accounts, and it happened more than the once.'

'But she must have reported what amounted to a violent seizure of her person, surely?' Rose protested. 'And if the master knew what had happened to her on one occasion, why did he allow her to be exposed to it again?'

Lily looked carefully around where they were sitting, then lowered her voice. 'The master can't be persuaded there's owt wrong with them,' she confided. 'To the master, they're just a bunch of spirited young bucks going off to bring lots of gold back to the country, and when they do they'll be rewarded with titles and suchlike.'

'So the master's never been present when any of these dreadful deeds have been committed — or even noticed their drunkenness and general debauchery?'

'No, not never,' Lily confirmed. 'Mind you, he keeps to himself in the other wing of the house. The one that looks like a church — that and the main hall, where he takes his meals with Father William.'

'Who's Father William?' Rose asked. 'I don't believe I've heard of him.'

'He came here a while ago,' Lily replied, 'and we only get to see him around suppertime, when he takes his one meal of the day with the master, then they pray together in the church in the east wing. So far as I can tell he's a priest, and the master seems to treat him like he's summat special. I heard them talking about how they weren't happy with the "Jesuits", and how they weren't doing enough to persuade the new king about something or other. Then they noticed I was listening to what they were saying, and they told me to leave, so I did. I wasn't interested anyroad, 'cos it was all about God, and I've got no time for that. It's not like when the master had the players up from London, and they were doing a masque all about St George and the dragon. Me and Mary sneaked up into that old loft above the main hall, where the musical folk used to sit in the old days, they reckon.'

'So there's a gallery over the main hall?' Rose asked, trying to keep any hint of real interest out of her voice.

Lily nodded. 'It's halfway up the wall on the far side, and the stairs that lead into it are behind a curtain in the service entrance. But the servants are strictly instructed not to go up there, and I don't reckon you'd be classed any different.'

'I wasn't thinking of going up there myself,' Rose lied. 'I was just curious, that's all. You don't get to see things like minstrel galleries in newly built halls like this one, and I'm surprised that someone as religious as the master would have much truck with wandering players and the like.'

'Well, you'd be wrong there,' said Lily. 'Visitors often call here, and the master lays on banquets and the like. You'll find out soon enough, when you have to do the cooking for them, 'cos it's always a big feast. Just a few weeks ago there was that lot from Derbyshire — the Countess of Shrewsbury, with a young lass who the master thinks should've been made queen when the last one died. That's what he said, anyroad, and I pretended I wasn't listening, in case I got told to leave again.'

In her next week as cook at Ollerton Hall, Rose had cause to put to use what she'd learned about the minstrels' gallery in the main hall. Word had come by way of the steward, Ralph Condor, that the master was expecting two important courtiers from London, one of whom was a baron of the realm who had occupied an important position in the administration of the late Queen Elizabeth. The master's instruction was to spare no expense for the banquet that was to be held in their honour, although the number sitting down to eat would be no more than four. Rose was instructed to prepare a list of what she proposed to serve, and two days before the anticipated arrival of these important visitors she received approval for the preparation and service of songbird pies, roast guinea fowl, venison, beef garlands, spiced lamprey, sugared almonds, marchpane frivols, and fruit tarts with honey sauce.

The banquet was well received by Markham and his guests, and Rose was summoned to the main hall to receive the personal congratulations of the handful who had partaken. She bowed and accepted the small bag of coins handed to her by the master. As she walked back out by way of the service entrance, she paused, pulled aside a wall hanging on the other side of the dividing curtain, and removed her leather pattens, so as to make no sound as she crept up the narrow stairway and into the minstrels' gallery.

She looked cautiously over the lip of the barrier, to remind herself of who was who, and in order to associate each voice she heard with the man who was speaking. It was not difficult, since the master's booming and commanding voice was familiar to her, while the man called Father William had the soft cadence of all priests ministering to their flock.

As for the two recent arrivals, she knew that they were brothers, and that their names were Brooke. The brief look she'd got of them as she stood politely receiving their praise had informed her that they were of approximately the same age, but that the one with the beard spoke with all the authority of an older sibling, though his manner of speech was more befitting of a wheedling courtier. His brother, on the other hand, sounded more like an old-fashioned country parson, with a louder voice accustomed to being listened to by a pliant congregation. To make matters easier as Rose ducked down below the ledge and out of sight, the older Brooke brother insisted on referring to the other as 'my younger brother'.

'Things appear to be proceeding in an excellent fashion,' the older man pronounced, 'and Thomas Grey will be well pleased. He looks askance at the number of those vile Scots who seem to have travelled south with the usurper in the hope of being awarded high office under his kingship, and the sooner we are able to disrupt their elevation the better. I have myself been in recent contact with those across the water, and we may confidently expect the Spanish money to be ready for me to collect following my next journey to the Low Countries. It will then be a simple matter of conveying it to Raleigh in Jersey. Do you have the men at arms that we shall require?'

'I will have shortly,' Markham replied confidently. 'My man Draycott has found a former soldier who is in the process of training that rabble from Sherwood who have proved so effective in tying up the town authorities and spreading chaos through the streets. You may take it from me that the people of Nottingham do not regard the accession year of James of Scotland as bringing about any improvement in their fortunes.'

'It's the same in other towns that we've been able to infect in a like manner,' the younger Brooke brother told him gloatingly. 'It has been my sole endeavour this past twelvemonth to ensure that the starving and desperate among the people of England are driven to extreme behaviour in the belief that they are in some way improving their lives, and those of their families.'

'This is all to the good,' observed the priest known as Father William. 'They are more inclined to cling to their faith in times of hardship, when they can be led gently towards the truth that their salvation may only be found in a return to the true religion. It is therefore a pity that Gerard and his acolytes do not deign to add their voice to the cry for a closer link with Rome, and that Blackwell's prepared to hold back simply because Garnet says so.'

'There's nothing we can do about that,' the elder Brooke brother reminded them, 'but they'll soon be knocking on our door seeking to do business when we have the usurper in our grasp. When we're in a position to dictate terms in return for the release of their Scottish fool, it will be ourselves who determine how fully we can re-open the realm for the Holy Father. And bear in mind that not all of our group are of a religious inclination — Baron Grey, as has already been mentioned, seeks merely to ensure that only English nobles grace the English court.'

'We are digressing,' said Markham. 'We must settle upon a time and place.'

It fell silent until the elder Brooke brother disclosed what he had in mind. 'The new king will be staying out of London for some time, for the plague has recently broken out there again. He is currently in Hertfordshire, at Theobalds House as the guest of the wretched Cecils. Once we are ready to strike, Raleigh proposes that we arrive there, or wherever else James might be by that date, pretending to present a petition. Our armed bands can take command for long enough for us to remove James to a place we have yet to determine, but most likely on the Welsh borders, from where we will dictate our terms for his return unharmed.'

'It's a bold plan,' Markham observed in a voice that, unusually for him, was somewhat tremulous.

'We need to be bold, Markham,' the elder Brooke brother insisted. 'These are crucial times, and if the true faith is to be restored to this realm, it must be done before a new monarch can continue the old blasphemies.'

'If we fail, we shall be dead men,' Markham reminded them.

'We shall be martyrs, you mean,' Father William replied quietly. 'Better to die in the comfort of the true faith than to continue in a life that places our souls in peril. Let us offer up a fervent prayer to God that our enterprise may thrive, with His blessing.'

While they were deep in prayer, Rose took the opportunity to slip down from her hiding place, put on her pattens and retire back to her kitchen. There she ensured that her staff were cleaning up after the massive banquet preparations, and were properly instructed as to which of the leftovers were to be served cold for supper. Then she retired for a brief rest in her room above the stables, trying to retain all she had overheard.

She had always been blessed with a detailed memory, which was what had enabled her, over the years, to absorb things she had been taught, by her mother and others, regarding the various uses to which herbs, spices and the many fruits of the land might be put. Now she concentrated hard on what she had overheard, in the hope of being able to relay it to Edward on his next visit to Ollerton.

There was some sort of plot against the throne, that was obvious, but the precise form that it was intended to take had not been made clear. So far as she could recall, a body of armed men — including those being trained by Edward — would be taken to wherever the new king could be found, and then he was to be seized and kept hidden away until the demands of the conspirators were met. These had something to do with religion, but what it was escaped her, since like Edward she had long since abandoned any interest in the Church and its false claims to goodness. The terrible treatment of young Annie was a fine example, conducted under the very nose of a self-proclaimed man of great piety.

Rose knew she would be of more use to Edward if she could learn more about those who had been conspiring during the banquet. With that objective in mind, she asked the steward if she might speak directly to the master regarding future meals, with particular reference to how long his guests might be staying. The ruse was successful, and late that afternoon, while supper was in the process of being prepared, she slipped out of the kitchen and was granted an audience with Markham. He sat before the empty fireplace in the main hall, stroking his two wolfhounds distractedly, and looking like a man who had dined too well to be fully alert.

'I hope you did not take offence at my effrontery in requesting to speak in person,' Rose began as she bowed, 'but I was overcome with pride at the praise you gave me for today's banquet, and I was hoping that I might be honoured to present more meals of that quality in the coming days. Please excuse my boldness, Master, but how long might your worthy guests be gracing us with their continued presence?'

'They will be departing the day after next,' Markham told her sleepily, 'since they have many important matters to supervise in connection with the future of the realm.'

'They are clearly both gentlemen of importance,' Rose replied in a tone that she hoped conveyed awe and admiration, playing on the master's vanity.

Markham sat back in his chair and began expanding on the quality of his connections. 'The two guests who so appreciated that excellent dinner are Henry and George Brooke. The older of the two — the one with the beard — is the eleventh Baron Cobham, and he enjoys a friendly relationship with Sir Walter Raleigh, one of our nation's greatest statesmen and heroes. He is about to embark on a voyage to the Americas, in search of a fabled city of gold, and the young adventurers who you see disporting themselves about my estate will form part of his entourage. They will return to England with more wealth than you could imagine in your fondest fantasies.'

'It must be so gratifying to be so well connected,' Rose replied encouragingly.

'There is also Thomas Grey,' Markham went on. 'His proper title is Baron Grey de Wilton, a great friend of the late Baron Burleigh and his son Robert Cecil, who governs the nation in the name of the new king. Baron Grey de Wilton is also a lifelong associate of the Brooke brothers, who are thereby drawn into the company of the Cecils. Robert Cecil is Secretary of State, in succession to his illustrious father who was so highly regarded by our late queen. But I must apologise if all this is somewhat distant from your own life, and perhaps tiresome to the ear.'

'Far from it, Master,' Rose replied as she committed all this to her capacious memory, 'although talking of my own life, there is a boon that I would seek, should it meet with your generous approval.'

'Pray simply ask, and if it be within my capacity, it shall be granted,' said Markham.

Rose assumed a pitiful expression. 'I shall of course remain at my post for as long as your illustrious guests continue to grace us with their presence. But once they have departed, might I be allowed to journey south to visit my younger sister, who is with child and expected to deliver within the next month or so? I have a little knowledge of physic, and she would deem it a great blessing were I able to visit and bring her such bodily comfort as she may require. As I assured you, it will not be until your visitors have departed. I will need no longer than one day, and I shall ensure that the kitchens are well stocked in advance.'

'Of course you may,' said Markham, 'and my grateful thanks for such devotion to your duties. But will you not require someone to accompany you, given the perilous nature of our country tracks?'

'I believe that Master Draycott might be persuaded to allow his warfare trainer to travel with me,' Rose replied.

'Excellent! See to whatever arrangements you need to make, and inform the steward that you have my leave to depart for two days rather than one.'

'You are most gracious, Master,' said Rose as she bowed from the presence, hoping that Edward would put in an appearance while her luck still held good.

As fate would have it, the following morning Lily told her that food would be required. 'We need to feed that bunch of vagabonds who've come from Sherwood with that handsome friend of yours. They're out in the bottom field, running up and down and pretending to be soldiers.'

It was time for Rose to seek out Edward and give him the excuse for accompanying her back south, assuming that Draycott would let him. Persuading Draycott might prove harder than getting two days off from Markham, but things had gone splendidly thus far, and Rose knew her potions. She grinned as the wicked thought entered her head, and she headed out to the stable yard in high spirits.

11

Edward stood to one side and gave the order for the dozen or so men he'd brought to Ollerton to begin the charge. They set off running and shouting, waving sticks and broom handles above their heads, and Edward cursed and yelled for them to stop. They did so in a ragged pattern that left half of them yards ahead of the others, and Edward called angrily for them to return to the starting point. Then he stalked across the coarse grass of the lower meadow and bellowed his displeasure.

'What was the first thing I taught you oafs? You!' he said to one of the youngest — the one who he'd hoped might one day become something approaching a man at arms.

The man looked shamefacedly back at him, then dropped his gaze to the grass as Edward pierced him with a glare.

'You don't charge like that, you ignorant fools!' Edward bellowed. 'Not with your arms above your heads, as if you were baling hay. You run forward with your swords at waist height, ready to parry enemy shields with your own, or cast them aside with an upward strike of your spare arm! If your arms are raised when you reach your target, you expose your own upper bodies to a blade from the enemy. You'd be dead before you even got to raise your own weapons! Now go back and do it again properly, you pathetic clods!'

He watched, fuming and cursing, as the men muttered among themselves. On his command, they began lurching across the uneven ground with about as much menace as young bullocks escaping from a tether. Edward looked away, disgusted and frustrated, in time to catch the amused grin of a finely dressed gentleman who'd left the bowls game on the upper green in order to scoff at the pathetic display.

'A shockingly ill-trained collection, are they not?' said the gentleman.

Edward glared back as he looked him up and down, taking in his fine blue cloak, his matching brown doublet and hose, and his polished black riding boots. 'And what would you know about swordplay?' he challenged him.

'I'd be able to acquit myself better than that,' the gentleman replied, nodding at the vagabond army. 'Which pig farm did you recruit them from?'

Edward felt a strong urge to punch the arrogant gentleman on the nose, but checked himself when he recalled that he was a house guest of Markham's. His mission for Cecil would end badly if he were ordered from the estate for striking a man who was seemingly highly regarded by the man that Edward had been commissioned to spy on. Instead he drew a deep breath and asked sarcastically, 'Perhaps you'd care to show them how it's done?'

'I could, had I a mind to it,' the gentleman replied, 'but I shall shortly be depriving Richard Lambert of more coin during our bowls contest in yonder meadow. Instead, I shall amuse myself for a few moments longer watching your clodhoppers attempting to imitate men at arms. You have my sympathy, but perhaps you might want to call them back, before they take root in the grass in which they seem to have planted themselves.'

Edward looked back out across their inadequate training ground. To his embarrassment and rage, his ramshackle group had seated themselves on the ground, some obviously needing to regain their breath. 'Get up and run back, in charge formation, to your original positions — *now!*' he snapped.

Edward heard the gentleman chuckle as the men heaved themselves to their feet and began lumbering back across the grass like cows in urgent need of milking, and he turned angrily. 'Pray tell me what justification you have for your demeaning manner towards those who are at least making the effort to become men at arms, while you fritter away your hours in idle gaming?'

'I am a soldier of fortune, sir,' the gentleman replied. 'Name of Howard de Vere, and I fought in Ireland alongside the Earl of Essex.'

'A futile campaign, as I heard,' Edward sneered. 'At least I had a leader worthy of respect — one whose men would have followed him through the very gates of Hell if so commanded. Had the Spanish reached London, as was their intent, they would have rued their impetuosity, and would all have perished on English blades.'

'You fought under Leicester?' de Vere asked, clearly impressed.

Edward nodded. 'In the event, we did not need to fight, because the Spaniards were put to flight at sea. But we were ready for them — five thousand of us, lined up at Tilbury, to hear Queen Elizabeth give us a speech of encouragement designed to stir the hearts of the most fearful. We stood and cheered her.'

'Very noble, I have no doubt,' de Vere commented in an offhand tone. 'I was one of those who deserted Essex after his own generals threatened to hang him high if he led us into one more ambush. I was not alone, either, should you judge me a coward. Those men you see rolling bowls across the grass because they have nothing more challenging to do were, in the main, my comrades in arms.'

'So you have a private army of sorts hidden away here?' Edward asked.

'We would have, were we inclined to seek reward or plunder. But we are promised much more in the way of wealth and fortune when we join Sir Walter Raleigh on his expedition to El Dorado. Those who currently occupy the city of gold can hardly be expected to yield it up meekly, so it shall be our task to persuade them that they may look forward to continued life only if they step aside while we fill our ships' holds.'

'And you think that to be an honourable quest, do you?' Edward challenged him.

De Vere turned away with a look of disdain. 'You can have all the honour you desire, in your company of peasants. It is gentlemen such as ourselves to whom the more important commodities of life are vouchsafed. And so I bid you a good day.'

Edward conducted the rest of the morning's exercises deep in thought. He was so engrossed in the implications of what he had learned from de Vere that he omitted to curse the bumbling efforts of the Sherwood recruits, even though there was no sign that by some miracle they were about to apply what they had been taught. He needed to alert the authorities to the fact that a private army was already assembled here, masquerading as a group of adventurers about to set sail in search of a fabled fortune in gold. Perhaps they actually believed that was their mission, and had somehow been duped into service under Markham in just the same way that Markham had prevailed upon Draycott to raise a body of fighting men, led by Edward. If Cecil's intelligence was to be believed — and given the tight deadline that Draycott had imposed on Edward to have the men battle-ready — then hidden away here in the north of Nottinghamshire was the beating heart of an impending challenge to the established order.

Edward had just set off hurriedly towards the main house in the hope of being able to make contact with Rose when he saw her beckoning to him from the doorway to the side of the building. He scurried over, and she hastened towards him with a broad smile. As they got closer, she began to speak in muted tones. 'Keep smiling, as if we were old friends meeting after a lengthy separation.'

'Is that not what we are anyway?' he replied.

'Of course, but we must pretend that our meeting is connected with the business that draws our two masters together, and not by prior arrangement. Your master is inside, conferring with my master by the fireplace in the main hall. They're casting furtive looks behind them as if anxious not to be overheard. And little wonder, given what I have learned about what is being hatched here. A plot against the throne, no less.'

'It is as Cecil suspected, and why I was sent here,' said Edward. 'I have just learned that these arrogant popinjays who appear to be house guests are in fact the first recruits for an armed force that is intended to bring about that uprising. You must impart what you have learned, then I must find an excuse to journey to Ashby without alerting suspicion.'

Rose laughed as she shook her head. 'There is far too much for me to be able to pass on during the brief conversation we are having, in which I am advising you that cheese and small beer awaits your men at the door to the stables. That is our excuse for this short meeting, should anyone enquire. But I have already obtained leave from my master to visit my sister who is with child, and to have you as my escort to preserve me from harm on my journey. All that it requires is the approval of

Master Draycott and we can set off tomorrow at first light. You will need to leave me at Daybrook and ride hard for the south, but it can be achieved, since Markham has granted me two days.'

'Would it not be best for you to give me the bare bones of what you have learned while we stand here?' Edward asked anxiously. 'It may be that I will not be granted leave to accompany you, and were I to do so without Draycott's blessing, he might become suspicious.'

'I've already advised you that there is insufficient time,' Rose replied as she nodded over Edward's shoulder. 'There is now no time left at all, for your master approaches.'

'He's *not* my master,' Edward growled as he turned and called out a greeting to Draycott.

Draycott looked far from pleased as he asked, 'Why are the men lying around the lower field like drunken day labourers at a country fair? Should you not be drilling them, or whatever it is you do?'

'They have just finished their training for the morning,' Edward assured him, 'and I was in the process of asking Mistress Middleham whether the men could be fed and watered.'

'And I have just advised him that the master has made generous provision for them to be served with bread, cheese and small beer,' Rose added. 'Will you be taking your dinner with the master? I have an excellent piece of pork that has been roasting since the sun first rose, and I shall be sending it upstairs as soon as I return from here. I feel sure that the master will not wish to dine alone now that his two guests have departed for their own homes.'

'I am indeed invited to stay to dinner,' Draycott said, puffing proudly, 'and I have heard that your cooking is unparalleled, so I shall look forward to sampling it.'

'You are most welcome,' Rose replied as she lowered her gaze and did her best to look embarrassed. 'In fact, the master was so appreciative of my humble efforts that he has graciously granted me leave to visit my sister in Arnold, and has been generous enough to allow me an escort against the perils of country lanes.'

'A very wise and generous gesture,' Draycott acknowledged.

Edward saw his opportunity. 'So you will not mind if I am that escort?' he asked.

Draycott frowned heavily. 'You are required back in Sherwood, to continue training the men. Did I not advise you that I need them to be ready within the month?'

'They will *never* be ready in such a short space of time, as I already advised you,' said Edward. 'It was agreed, was it not, that I would simply arrange for them to *appear* to be fighting men?'

'So it was,' Draycott conceded, 'but how can I be assured that you will return after escorting this lady to her sister's house? After all, you joined us with reluctance, so you might take this opportunity to slip away.'

'I joined you because I had nowhere else to go,' said Edward, 'and it was I who brought Mistress Middleham into our fold. You were then able to introduce her to Sir Griffin, thereby adding to his high opinion of you. Why should either of us wish to leave the company in which we have both found such sanctuary?'

Draycott considered that argument for a moment, then narrowed his eyes as he came to a decision. 'I shall not seek to prevent you from ensuring this good lady's safety as she makes her family visit, but it shall be on the condition that I accompany you both, thereby ensuring your return.'

Edward was hastily searching for some objection to an arrangement that would not only prevent him journeying on to Ashby, but would also reveal the presence, in Daybrook, of County Bailiff Francis Barton. But to his surprise and disappointment, Rose clapped her hands in delight.

'You are *most* gallant, sir, and I shall of course gratefully accept the protection of *two* such brave and worthy gentlemen. But I am keeping you from your dinner. Pray accompany me inside, and Master Mountsorrel may call for us here at daybreak. No doubt my master will be gracious enough to allow you to bide here overnight, and for Edward it will be but a short journey from Sherwood in the dawn light.'

Edward was about to protest until Rose shot him a warning glance out of the corner of her eye. Then, when Draycott's back was turned, she whispered, 'Leave him to me,' before scuttling back towards the scullery door.

Edward spent a restless night wrapped in his cloak, sleeping outside the wooden shack that was now his official residence. His excuse for doing so was the fact that Janey was still not fully healed and would be likely to keep him awake with her occasional whimpers.

Far from refreshed, he stirred himself as he saw the grey light appear through the treetops. By the time the grey had become a pale pink, he was trotting the borrowed horse towards the scullery door, where Rose was awaiting him, clutching a travel bag and holding a horse by the bridle. Edward was intrigued to glimpse men's hose peeping out below the hem of her gown. He was also both puzzled and relieved to note that she was alone.

'Where is Draycott?' he asked.

She giggled. 'In the jakes, for the next two days or so. I knew that the greedy old soak would take every opportunity to imbibe at the master's expense, so I took it upon myself to serve them both generously with wine. I added a few herbs to Draycott's cup, and within the hour he was making his excuses and scuttling from the dining table as if pursued by demons. He will be squirting out his penance for at least the remainder of today, and will not wish to undertake any journey on the back of a horse. So let us be away without delay, in case he bids us wait until he has regained the ability to fart without soiling his hose.'

'Remind me never to give you any cause for anger,' Edward chuckled as he gave Rose a lift into the saddle, then swung up onto the back of his own mount.

They trotted sedately down the drive, Rose riding demurely in the sideways style of all ladies until they reached the main track that led from Ollerton, south towards Bilsthorpe. Then she slid from the sideways saddle and unstrapped it before concealing it in the hedgerow to the side of the track. Hitching up her skirts to reveal most of the rest of her hose, she jumped back onto the horse, legs astride its bare back in the manner of a horseman. As she kicked its sides to encourage it to move faster, Edward called out to her in alarm.

'Do you intend to journey all the way to Daybrook in that fashion?'

'Clearly I do. We will make much faster time if I am not riding like some performer in a sideshow, and you need to journey on to Ashby, do you not? I have been riding bareback, in the manner of a humble man at arms, since I was seven years old. Let us pick up the pace while I tell you what I have learned.'

By the time they reached Daybrook, with the sun just beginning to descend from its full height, Edward had absorbed all that Rose could tell him regarding what she'd overheard while hiding in the minstrels' gallery. The clear threat of treason needed to be relayed to Cecil without delay.

Rose and Kitty embraced lovingly in the manner of devoted sisters, while Edward shared what he had learned with Francis while hastily gobbling some bread and cheese, which he washed down with a large mug of Kitty's home-brewed apple cider. Then he retrieved his own horse from the stable in which Francis had been caring for him and rode hard to Ashby, making use of his intimate knowledge of the country tracks around Beeston and Sawley, and the ferry over the Trent at Wilden, in order to quicken his journey and avoid the centre of Nottingham.

Even so, it was fully dark when he hitched his horse to the post outside the Porters' cottage and removed his muddy boots. He crept through the main room of the house, where his children were fast asleep in front of the embers of a dying fire, and into the main bedchamber. He shed his clothing, then slipped beneath the bedding and enfolded a sleeping Elizabeth in his arms. His actions half woke her, and she turned her head to enquire groggily, 'Is that you, Edward, or am I having a pleasant dream?'

'It is I, true enough,' he replied, 'and you may add this to your dream.' He raised the hem of her nightdress in anticipation.

12

The long journey, and the sleepless night ahead of it, had taken their toll on Edward. When he awoke, it was to the shock of his three delighted children jumping on the bed and calling, 'Daddy!' He rolled over, realised that the sun was already up, and yelled at the children to go back into the main room while he grabbed the clothing he'd cast onto the floor.

'They're just happy to see you,' Elizabeth chided him from the doorway, 'as am I. Now finish getting dressed and come through for the breakfast that I've prepared, and tell me all your news.'

'I've no time for that!' Edward snapped. 'I must take myself up the drive to the castle to pass on what I've learned to the Earl of Huntingdon in order that it may be relayed to Cecil in London as a matter of urgency. There's a threat to the throne!'

'There's also a threat to our marriage if you don't come through and eat, and at least pretend that you wish to spend time with your wife and children. Can you not spare us all another day at least?'

'I really cannot,' Edward said, his heart in his boots as he saw the pain in Elizabeth's eyes. 'I must pass on what I know to the earl, then I must ride back to Daybrook, collect Rose and ensure that we both show our faces back in Ollerton before sunset.'

Elizabeth let out a terrible oath, then stormed out of the bedchamber into the main room, shouting, 'The worthless rat is leaving again — God curse the day that I ever fell for his false charms! Eat your breakfast, children, and do not bother to wish your father Godspeed, for he does not deserve either your concern or the name of "father". Now go, Edward, and think hard on your loyalties as you ride away yet again. Is it me you wish to please, or that Devil's servant — that murderer of marriages — Cecil?'

There was clearly no point in attempting to mount a spirited defence, despite the injustice of the accusations. Edward was already late for what he had to do next, so with mumbled apologies to the assembled company in the main room, which included a distressed and embarrassed-looking Edwin and Catherine Porter, he strode outside and saddled up.

As he cantered up the long drive to Ashby Castle, he tried to forget the heart-wrenching scene he'd left behind by taking in his immediate surroundings, and one building in particular caught his attention. It sat in a small cottage garden of its own, surrounded by a low yew hedge that was clearly intended to afford it some privacy, yet it seemed uninhabited. A wild idea was forming in his mind as he hastily dismounted, threw his horse's bridle in the direction of the sleepy-looking stable groom who appeared from nowhere, then strode purposefully through the imposing front door and into the main entrance hall.

There was movement to the left, and a well-dressed middle-aged man who gave the appearance of being the current steward walked through a doorway and demanded to know his business.

'I need to speak to your master without delay,' Edward announced.

The man looked him up and down with a suspicious frown. 'And who might you be?'

'Edward Mountsorrel, bailiff to the Sheriff of Nottingham.'

'This is Leicestershire,' said the man.

Edward cursed softly. 'I am well aware of the layout of this part of the nation, you buffoon, but I am not here on mere town business. I come from Robert Cecil, Secretary of State, and I must speak with Sir George without delay.'

'He is at breakfast,' the steward told him.

'Then pray announce my intention of joining him, since I have not eaten since noon yesterday, such is the urgency of my business. Tell him that the life of the new king is under threat, and that he will forfeit his own if he does not relay what I have to tell him to London without delay.'

That seemed to achieve the desired result, and two minutes later the elegantly attired master of the house looked up from his well-stocked board with a frown.

'Your face is familiar,' he remarked, 'but I am surprised that you are authorised to use the name of Cecil in order to gain admission. Would you care to join me at board?'

'I will, and gladly, once I have imparted the news I wish to have relayed down to Secretary Cecil in London,' Edward replied as he took a seat.

The earl frowned. 'I was told that you came *from* Cecil, not that you wished to communicate *with* him. Now I remember where I have seen your face before — you came here on a prior occasion pretending to be someone you were not.'

'I was mistaken for someone else,' Edward reminded him hotly, 'and you consigned me to a dungeon below ground until my true identity was revealed to you, along with my real purpose for being here. Your apology then was most contrite, but it clearly had a limited lifespan. Now, is it not the case that Secretary Cecil entrusted you with the grave duty of passing on such intelligence that might be brought to you regarding any planned plot against the Crown?'

'He did indeed,' the earl confirmed, 'and he also named the man who would be bringing it to me. So reveal your identity, if you would be so obliging.'

'Edward Mountsorrel, bailiff to the Sheriff of Nottingham.'

'That is who I was told to expect. Now pray help yourself to some of this excellent manchet, along with a portion of the cheese, which is a local speciality.'

'I cannot speak with a mouth full of food,' Edward pointed out, 'and I must incur no more delay in imparting what I have learned. There is a plot against the life of our new king, which is to come to fruition when a group of traitors from the north of Nottingham approach him under the guise of presenting a petition.'

'Nottingham?' the earl repeated. 'Not Derbyshire?'

'It may well involve the Lady Arbella Stuart,' said Edward, 'but of that I cannot yet be certain. What I *do* know is that the house of one Sir Griffin Markham is being used as a rallying point for a body of soldiers of fortune who either believe, or are pretending, that they are assembling ahead of joining the courtier Walter Raleigh on an expedition to find a city of gold in the New World.'

'Ah, Raleigh again,' the earl continued. 'Cecil was wise to be suspicious of the man's restored favour at court. But he is currently abroad, is he not?'

'In Jersey, as I learned. But he is apparently to be in receipt of funds to raise an army against the new king. The money is to come from Spain through the agency of some nobleman whose name escapes me. It is expected to be delivered shortly, and the private army being amassed by Markham will be employed to capture the king and hold him to ransom until certain demands are met. I believe these to be connected with the restoration of the Catholic Church here in England, for there is also a man in residence in Ollerton who calls himself Father William. He seems to be a priest who conducts clandestine Masses for Markham.'

The earl thought for a moment, then nodded. 'That is no doubt the secular priest known to us as William Watson, who is currently at odds with the Jesuits. It was the Jesuits who first warned Cecil that the secular party might be planning some sort of scheme against the planned coronation of King James, until they had secured certain assurances from him regarding the celebration of Mass and other Popish indulgences. Watson was imprisoned for some time during the reign of the late queen, but found favour with James of Scotland when he was released on the condition that he and his faction would support his claim to the English throne. He repays such kindness very poorly. As for Raleigh, he would seem to have a death wish.'

'Is he not one of our nation's heroes?' Edward asked. 'I heard much of his exploits during my days in armed service under the Earl of Leicester, and seemingly he was one of the late queen's favourites at court. Does he not wish to lend his loyal support to the man who Elizabeth nominated as her heir?'

'You are guilty of several assumptions there, my friend,' said the earl. 'The first is regarding whether or not James really was Her Majesty's choice to inherit her throne. There are, as you will be aware, several others who might have been considered, including the lady from Derbyshire.'

'She visited Ollerton recently,' Edward told him. 'At least, that is what my spy inside the house was able to glean from conversations to which she was secretly privy. But you say that I was also wrong regarding the loyalty of this man Raleigh?'

'Let me advise you of certain matters pertaining to Sir Walter. First of all, he is a man with great imagination, considerable charm and breeding, but no common sense. Despite having wormed his way into Her Majesty's innermost circle by observing her love of flattery, he completely overlooked her likely reaction should he give the impression that another woman occupied a greater position in his heart than she. He secretly married one of her ladies, Bess Throckmorton, and they were both thrown into the Tower. They were fortunate to keep their heads, such was Elizabeth's rage. Yet somehow he managed to worm his way back into public office.'

'No doubt with the promise that he would bring great riches back to England from this fabled city of gold?' Edward suggested.

The earl let out a derisive laugh. 'Let me advise you of certain *other* facts regarding Raleigh. This fabled city of gold has been an obsession of his for over ten years. He uses the promise of great riches to persuade others to finance voyages across to the New World, taking great care never to embark himself. He has already lost one group of settlers in an attempt to form a colony in a place they called Roanoke. They might have been spared from starvation, or whatever fate may have befallen them, had he sent ships with further supplies, as they were promised. Instead he loaned his ships to Queen Elizabeth when the Spanish threatened to invade, thereby further winning her favour while condemning his colonists. It was shortly after that when he disgraced himself with that unfortunate marriage to which I referred earlier, but then he secured his release by offering to organise pirate fleets, one of which captured a Spanish carrack called the *Madre de Deus*, which was laden with gold. His return to royal favour was then assured, once again without him ever risking his life at sea. He has since taken to boasting that he will sail to the Spanish coast of the Americas, claiming that he knows where the city of gold may be located. By this means he amasses finance from willing investors, while attracting young noblemen with no prospects — third and fourth sons, in the main — for some purpose which you may have helped to reveal. They are tilting to place the English crown in safe Catholic hands.'

'So Raleigh is a secret Catholic?'

'Far from it.' The earl almost spat in the rushes. 'Were he a devotee of Rome, he would not have wormed his way so successfully into the late queen's affections. You will not find a more staunchly Protestant family in the whole of England than the Raleighs, and his mother's family, the Champernownes. No, sir, Raleigh is little more than a high-born mountebank who seeks office and advancement by means of wild promises and romantic speculations that he is in no position to fulfil. But if there be any justice in this world, he has outreached even himself this time. The Cecils have long suspected him of disloyalty to the throne, and will need little persuasion that he has made himself the paymaster for an armed uprising. I shall of course relay everything you have told me down to London without delay. But before I do, can you give me the names of any others who are part of this wicked intrigue?'

Edward thought long and hard, then remembered something else that Rose had recounted. 'There are two brothers, one of whom is a baron of the realm. They were visiting Markham during my time at Ollerton, and I believe their names to be "Brooke", or something similar.'

The earl paled slightly as he sought further clarification. 'Not by any chance Henry Brooke, Baron Cobham, and his younger brother Sir George Brooke, himself a clergyman?'

'I believe that those were the names,' Edward confirmed. 'Why do you look askance at me — have I disclosed something that displeases you?'

'Not half as much as it will displease Sir Robert Cecil,' the earl replied with a grimace. 'He was once married to their sister Elizabeth. She died some years ago, leaving him with a son and a daughter, both still in infancy. But he will not take kindly to having anyone remember that he was once the brother-in-law of two conspirators who are seeking to depose the man Cecil has worked tirelessly to place on the throne.'

Edward let out a hollow laugh. 'I myself had cause to fall foul of one of his schemes to ingratiate himself with the Scots king, as he then was.'

'And still is,' the earl added. 'There is talk that our new king seeks to make one nation out of England and Scotland. This is, of course, another reason why some may be seeking to replace him as king.'

'What further action do you require of me?' Edward asked hesitantly. 'I was rather hoping that I might remain here in Ashby. My wife and children are currently occupying the grace-and-favour cottage that was once the old lodge gatehouse, since it was given to my father-in-law to occupy when he retired as the previous estate steward. My wife is again with child, and I would welcome the opportunity to either be at her side here in Ashby, or return with her to our house in Nottingham.'

The earl shook his head sympathetically. 'It is essential that you return to the house of this man Markham, around whom the treasonous plot seems to have flourished. We need to learn when the plot has been unleashed, which by my guess will be indicated by the departure of those who are assembled there to travel to London, or wherever the king may be found. Can you undertake to let us know of this without delay?'

'Of course,' Edward replied unhappily. 'I gave Cecil my word. I am sworn to uphold the law of the realm in my office as town bailiff, and there can be no peace if men such as myself shirk their responsibilities.'

'A pretty speech,' the earl commented, 'and I mean nothing demeaning by that. Would that every man could honour his duties so steadfastly. But in return, what might I do for your wife and family while you are away from them?'

Edward pressed home the advantage. 'On my short journey up the drive from the former gatehouse, my eye fell upon a substantial dwelling, one of perhaps six rooms. It was surrounded by a delightful and well-tended garden, but it appeared to be unoccupied. You are of course aware of it?'

'Naturally, since it is designated as the "dower house". It is currently empty, due to the fact that there is no dowager countess in need of it. If I understand where your question is leading, would you be content for your family to move in there, to await the impending birth of which you spoke? I can have men arrange to make it more habitable, and no doubt someone may be spared from my kitchens to see to your family's daily needs. In due course I could also provide them with the services of a midwife from the village who ministered to my own wife during her several lyings-in. If you find this proposal acceptable...?'

'Indeed I do, and I thank you for your generosity and understanding,' Edward beamed. 'Now, might I withdraw in order to pass on the news of your largesse to my wife, ahead of riding back to Ollerton?'

He was allowed to leave only after he had availed himself of a late breakfast, but an hour later he was dismounting once again outside the Porters' cottage.

Edwin Porter appeared in the doorway with a frown. 'Elizabeth has spent the morning in tears,' he growled. 'Can you not ride on?'

'I cannot,' Edward insisted, 'since I have hopeful news for her. She and the children are granted leave to move into the dower house.'

'What's a "dower house"?' his daughter Margaret asked as she appeared from behind her grandfather's back. 'And are you going to make Mama cry again?'

'She cannot cry any more, since she has already used up a year's tears,' said Elizabeth as she pushed past both of them to stand defiantly in front of the door. 'Are you here for long enough to make more pathetic noises and perhaps fill your stomach, before finding a lame excuse to ride off alone?'

'I must certainly ride off within the hour,' Edward conceded, 'but I bring good news. The Earl of Huntingdon has graciously granted you leave to occupy the dower house that you no doubt remember from your childhood. It lies just up the lane there, and has enough room for two families. The earl will also supply a midwife for your lying-in.'

'Because you will not be here in person?' she replied tartly. 'And if you are not here, who will defend us from those who might seek to rob and pillage a fine house of its contents?'

'I thought perhaps the Bailiff of Nottinghamshire,' Edward replied as inspiration struck.

Elizabeth frowned. 'Why would Francis consent to desert his own wife and son, when she is also expecting a child?'

'I had in mind that they *all* remove themselves down here, at least temporarily,' Edward explained. 'They may also bring with them Kitty's sister Rose, who is skilled in all manner of physic, but particularly childbirth.'

'I suppose that having company around me will in some ways compensate for your continued absence,' said Elizabeth with no obvious pleasure in her face. 'So when will all this be taking place?'

'If you make application to the earl's steward, he will make arrangements to see to your transfer, along with the children, and indeed your parents, should you so wish. As for Francis, Kitty and Rose, I must ride back north and request that they lose no time in joining you down here.'

'And if they decline?'

'They will not, trust me in that,' Edward assured her.

She shrugged, then forced a smile to her lips. 'Is there not something you require before you leave?'

Edward shook his head. 'I have partaken of breakfast at the earl's table.'

'I had in mind my blessing, and my apology for my harsh words earlier,' Elizabeth replied as she forced back yet more tears. 'At least come over here and kiss me goodbye.'

He did as requested, and felt agonies of regret as she hugged him tightly and whispered, 'You are the most infuriating, unreliable and errant man that a woman ever had the misfortune to wed, but I would not have wished for any other. Come back safely.'

13

'You missed the sight of my wife having a wash,' Francis commented sardonically as he watched Edward dismount outside the Daybrook house. 'If you are staying until tomorrow, you might enjoy greater fortune, although there is much more to her than there was last time.'

'I sometimes wonder why I married you,' said Kitty as she appeared behind him in the doorway, with little Richard clinging to her skirts.

'For the very reason why you have one child beside you, and another in your belly,' Francis joked, then ducked in time to miss the hand aimed at the back of his head. Then he turned back to Edward.

'You did not, however, miss supper, so come away in and let us enjoy one more repast prepared by Rose before you take her away again.'

'A hasty change of plan,' Edward told him. 'Not regarding supper, however, so lead the way, although I am bound to advise you that I breakfasted with the Earl of Huntingdon. I was then treated to some cold tongue from my wife before I took my leave after less than one day back in Ashby.'

'How fares Elizabeth?' Kitty asked as they sat around the supper table. 'I hope that she is not plagued with the same aching back that I must suffer, and without the simples from Rose that ease the suffering.'

'The only thing she complains about is my absence,' Edward replied, 'and she will shortly be moving into the old dower house on the Ashby estate along with the children. The earl was most generous when I was able to advise him of the plot that is being hatched back in Ollerton, for which of course I am indebted to Rose.'

'I am most reluctant to return with you,' Rose muttered. 'Apart from the dismal company that is to be found there, I am apprehensive about leaving Kitty so close to her lying-in.'

'What if I were to advise you that you need not do so?' Edward asked.

Kitty placed her hands together in mock prayer. 'Please God you are not jesting.'

'I would not jest regarding something so serious,' Edward assured her. 'But as you reminded us, you are not the only one approaching childbirth. I seek Rose's agreement to transfer herself, together with yourself and Richard, down to Ashby, there to await the two births under the careful gaze of an experienced midwife.'

'Leaving me alone here?' Francis asked as he put down the paring knife with which he had just helped himself to another slice of pickled pork.

Edward shook his head. 'It is my further proposal that you accompany them down there, and be in attendance when the births occur, guarding the entire household.'

'Now you *are* jesting,' Francis said, raising his eyebrows.

'I have never been more serious,' said Edward.

Kitty turned to fix Francis with a stern glare. 'If you seek to dissuade him, you will find me less eager regarding wifely service.'

'Heaven forfend,' Francis replied, although his face reflected his reservations.

It fell silent until Rose asked, 'If I do not return to Ollerton, who will be your eyes and ears?'

'We no longer have need of them,' Edward explained, 'since we already know what is afoot. Thanks to you, Cecil can prepare for the arrival at court of Markham and his treasonous band. What is needed now is someone who can alert the authorities when they depart on their way south, and that is something I can do myself, either in person or by way of a messenger.'

'How can I be your messenger, if I am guarding the house in Ashby?' Francis asked. 'And before we descend into any further discussion of this madcap proposal, pray tell me how I am to conduct my many duties as bailiff for three sheriffs in your absence?'

'Do each of them complain that you neglect your duties for them while carrying out the wishes of the others?' Edward asked.

'What do *you* think?' Francis replied hotly. 'They are each convinced that I have been bribed by the others. Littlefare and Hynde complain ceaselessly that I cannot give the town the same undivided attention that you once did, while Rayner has formed the belief that I have deserted his service entirely.'

'Then none of them is likely to notice your additional absence,' Edward argued. 'You need only show your face on, say, one day per week, dividing your time between the Guildhall and Daybrook, and leave the real work to your senior constables, swearing them to silence regarding your extended leave of absence. Although while I think about it, you will be one constable less, since I will need a messenger to send south to Ashby, should I be required to travel south with the main party.'

'It gets worse!' Francis grumbled.

Kitty placed a hand firmly on his arm. 'Mind my warning about seeking to dissuade him. And would you not wish to have Rose in attendance when the latest Barton sees the light of day?'

'Of course, but my concern is regarding the need to absent myself from my duties. I cannot be sure that my senior constables will be up to the task of holding down the peace in my absence, particularly not if Edward is insisting on taking one of the town hands with him.'

'Not only do you overestimate your own value to the justice network,' Edward said with a laugh, 'but you undervalue the ability of those you have trained to work under you. And let me remind you that something of far greater importance is involved here — something that pertains to the welfare and stability of the entire nation. Once Cecil lets it be known that we were both acting in his name, the sheriffs will be only too pleased to overlook any temporary reduction in your activities. And would you leave our families exposed to evil?'

'They will surely be safe enough in the grounds of Ashby manor,' Francis grumbled.

Kitty moved away from him and gave him a hard stare. 'And you are prepared to take that risk, are you?' she demanded.

Francis had no argument against that, and instead asked Edward which of the town constables he had in mind.

Edward saw another opportunity to expose Francis to emotional blackmail. 'Do you recall that when I was striving to prove your innocence after you were accused of murdering the Widow Timberlake, I employed the local carter's son, one Robbie Bishop, to guard our chief witness in your defence, Mary Blythe?'

'I am hardly likely to forget it,' Francis conceded grumpily, 'but what of it?'

'Robbie turned out to have the strength of an ox and the courage of a wolf defending its young,' Edward continued, 'and I recruited him into the town force as Constable Bishop. Have you come across him?'

'I believe I have,' said Francis. 'He's a mountain of a man with a shock of red hair. His wife often comes to meet him from the Guildhall in order to prevent him visiting the alehouse with the other constables when their duties are at an end. She's a large woman with a birthmark on one cheek.'

'You have a short memory as far as she is concerned,' Edward observed. 'She is — or rather was — the same Mary Blythe who worked as Widow Timberlake's maid, and was able to advise your trial jury that you had been rendered insensible with a potion while others were let into the house in order to take her mistress's life. You must surely remember her as the girl in service to the lady who was at that time your — your great friend.' He managed to convey the impression that if pushed to it, he would reveal to Kitty and Rose how precisely that 'friendship' had been conducted.

Francis took the hint. 'Yes, I remember Mary Blythe, but again, what of it?'

'She is now Mary Bishop, and Robbie is greatly indebted to me for encouraging their relationship and appointing him to a post in which he could provide enough financial security to raise their children. There were four of them, at the last count.'

'And?' Francis pressed him.

Edward smiled. 'Prior to departing for Ashby, I wish you to remind him of his debt to me, and instruct him to take my horse from the stable here, then ride him to Sherwood and seek the camp currently occupied by those who Draycott placed in my charge to be trained as soldiers. The story he is to tell is that he robbed and murdered a man in Bellar Gate and stole his horse in order to escape justice. He will of course not reveal that he and I are acquainted, and he may then join the armed band that I am training, and will be allowed to keep his horse — *my* horse — on the pretence that I am seeking to add cavalry to our force. When Markham and his party depart south — with me among them — he can ride hard to Ashby and alert you. You in turn can alert the Earl of Huntingdon, and by his hand word can be relayed to Cecil, who will no doubt already be in attendance on the king.'

'You have a very detailed plan conceived,' Francis observed, 'any part of which may easily go awry. In the meantime, I am doing nothing except guarding three women and what will in due course be six children.'

'You find such a task beneath you?' Rose asked sharply.

'Have a care how you answer,' Kitty added.

The following morning, Edward climbed back onto the borrowed horse and took the road north, back to Sherwood in the hope that he could convincingly explain Rose's absence. He consoled himself with the reassurance that he had done all he could for Elizabeth's ongoing welfare, as well as that of Kitty, Rose and the children, while not abandoning his responsibilities. He was half a day late in returning, but hopefully this would add some credibility to the story he'd composed to explain Rose's absence.

'You were supposed to be back here yesterday,' Draycott reminded Edward accusingly as he dismounted outside the wooden shack that was notionally his. 'And where's the cook you were supposed to be escorting?'

'That's why I'm a trifle delayed,' Edward explained as he tried his best to look crestfallen and fearful. 'She slipped away during the night, and I spent half a day looking for her, but in vain.'

'Sir Griffin will be extremely displeased,' Draycott said with a frown, 'and it's just another example of how useless you are. While you were away, one of Sir Griffin's guests who has experience with arms was asked to take over the training of the men you were supposed to be turning into an armed band. He reported back to Sir Griffin that they'd been badly instructed, and were fit only for shovelling dung from his stables. He's not best pleased, and neither am I, so look to your duties, otherwise you'll no longer be sleeping in this fleapit of a hut. You might even be invited to leave the camp.' With that, he strode away with a look of disgust.

Janey, who'd been standing outside their hut listening to the conversation, sidled up to Edward and placed her arms around him consolingly, releasing a waft of stale sweat from her armpits. Edward tried not to gag as she said, 'Never mind, lovey. Thanks to your friend and her potions I'm not feeling any more pain, so you and me can finally enjoy each other once it gets dark. Come in and I'll give you some of the coney stew left over from yesterday.'

'I need to speak to my men first,' Edward insisted as he forced himself to look appreciative. 'Draycott tells me that they're not up to the mark, so I'll need to get them off their arses and back into shape. That may take a while, so I'll get back when I can.'

With that he turned and strode purposefully into the centre of the camp clearing, calling for the men he'd been training to come out and line up in front of him. They did so with their customary slovenly resentment.

'You're a poor show, according to the man who was training you in my absence!' Edward said. 'Let's see what we can do to improve his opinion of you all, shall we?'

'Why should we be seeking the good opinion of *him*?' one of the men replied. There were shouts of agreement from the rest of the group.

Edward sensed that all had not gone well while he'd been away, and decided to probe a little further. 'Which of them was it?' he asked.

It fell silent for a moment until Tom Maunder, the young man for whom Edward held out some hope as a man at arms, replied, 'He said his name was de Vere, and he claims he fought against the Irish when he was a soldier under the Earl of Essex.'

'Ah yes, Howard de Vere,' Edward confirmed. 'He already gave me the benefit of his opinion of you lot as a fighting force, and right now I'm inclined to agree with him. But God help me, I've been blighted with the task of turning you into an armed band.'

'At least you don't call us "useless lumps of dog dirt", like *he* did,' Tom muttered. 'And he didn't seem to have much idea when it comes to sword-fighting, anyroad. We learned more from you in one hour than he taught us in half a day.'

'So are you prepared to knuckle down and work twice as hard under my instruction?' Edward asked, and a rousing cheer assured him that they were.

He drilled them remorselessly until the sun had been down for several hours, taking advantage of the full moon to get them practising the swordplay actions that he'd been instilling into them. Apart from ensuring that they'd been through those actions so often, and so thoroughly, that they'd become instinctive, he'd hopefully delayed his return to the hut for so long that Janey would have succumbed to sleep. To his intense relief his guess was proved correct, and after pulling the blanket off the grazing horse that had recently borne him down to Ashby and back, he curled up under the overhanging branches of a sturdy oak tree and fell asleep.

He was awoken by the sensation of someone kicking the soles of his boots. When he stirred and turned over, he was met with the sight of Draycott glowering down at him.

'Off your arse and see to this latest recruit for what passes for your army,' he was instructed.

He raised himself up on one elbow and looked past Draycott to where Robbie Bishop was standing, holding Edward's horse by its guiding rein. 'Who's he?' he asked.

'He claims that his name's Robbie Blythe, and that he's on the run from the authorities after he robbed and killed a man in the town, then stole his horse. He's asking to join us, and the horse looks useful, so do what you can with him. I'm due up at Ollerton Hall, so I'll leave him to you.'

Draycott walked away, leaving Edward to rise to his feet and saunter over to where Robbie Bishop stood grinning at him, still holding the horse.

'Take that stupid grin off your face!' Edward instructed him sharply, then looked him up and down. Robbie had clearly dressed for the part. Edward had never seen him look so grubby and ill clad, with dirty mud-stained hose and boots, and what looked like half a dead sheep covering a heavily stained undershirt.

'Robbie Blythe — is that your name?' Edward demanded.

Fortunately, Robbie seemed to get the message as he nodded and replied, 'Yes, but mebbe I should use another one, 'cos half the town's looking for me after I killed a mark I was trying to rob. He shouldn't have put up a fight, stupid bastard.'

'Well, you came to the right place,' Edward assured him as he absentmindedly fondled the horse's mane. The horse gave a friendly whinny and snuggled his head into Edward's shoulder. 'When did you last eat?'

'Can't remember,' Robbie replied.

Edward nodded towards the shack occupied by Janey and her two children. 'Go into that shambles and ask the woman called Janey for some of her coney stew. You can tell her that I sent you. When you've eaten, come and join the men. I'll be teaching them how to wield a sword. You're a strapping-looking lad, so maybe we can find a use for you. But I'll keep the horse for the time being.'

In due course Robbie took his place among the men that Edward was drilling, and it was obvious that he was much fitter than the rest of them. The men looked apprehensively at his sheer bulk and mean facial expression as they went through the 'cut', 'parry' and 'thrust' drill yet again, in between bouts of running on the spot, or racing from one side of the clearing to the other.

The sun was well past its high point as Edward became aware of the return of Draycott, who was deep in conversation with one of the older men in the camp who had not been deemed suitable for arms training. Edward noted the frown on Draycott's face as the two men stood watching the group exercises, and after a while he walked over to Edward with an angry expression.

'Markham threw a fit when he learned that he no longer has a cook, and he requires your attendance at the Hall in order to explain yourself. I'm to take you over there without delay.'

'I need to finish drilling the men,' Edward objected.

Draycott's heavy hand landed on his shoulder. 'I said *without delay*, so go and get that horse that you've obviously taken a great liking to. I don't take kindly to being kept waiting, any more than Markham does.'

An hour later they were walking towards the front entrance to Ollerton Hall. Draycott veered off to the left, towards the scullery door, and told Edward to go straight into the main building without him.

'In the absence of the cook who you succeeded in losing, they're back to serving pigswill in there, as I discovered when I dined with Markham earlier today. As a result I'm still hungry, so in you go, and I'll join you in a short while.'

Edward did as instructed, but was held back by Steward Condor, who left him standing in the entrance hall for a considerable time before he was invited to push open the two heavy doors that led into the main hall, where Markham was waiting for him.

But he was not alone. Edward was just asking himself whether Draycott had eaten sufficient before deciding to join Markham when the latter barked out an instruction.

'Stay right there and cast off your sword belt.'

Surprised and a little apprehensive, Edward did as instructed, and allowed both the belt and the sword to clatter down onto the flagstones. Markham nodded, then turned to indicate Draycott to his left.

'Master Draycott has reason to believe that you've been sent to spy on us. I'd prefer not to believe that, but if it's true then you clearly cannot be allowed to mix freely with us any longer.'

'I can assure you that I haven't,' Edward insisted as nervous bile rose towards his throat.

Draycott was looking triumphant as he made a noise that sounded like a pig's bladder being flattened and waved an accusing finger at Edward. 'You over-reached yourself by bringing that fat man into the company, and pretending that you didn't know him. I was surprised, and a little suspicious, when I saw how that horse he brought with him reacted to you, suggesting that you and it had met before. Then one of the camp's oldest residents, who's made several unsuccessful attempts to enter Nottingham by night, told me that he knew the man calling himself "Robbie Blythe" from previous encounters. He can hardly be mistaken for anyone else, given his size. My man tells me that he's a town constable who's booted his arse more than once, and sent him back here with a sore head. I think you would agree that the coincidence is too great — a man claiming to be a disgraced and dismissed town bailiff, and a man who, for all we know, is still a serving town constable. You've been sent to spy on us, have you not?'

'I have not,' Edward insisted, 'and until this moment I was not aware that there was anything going on here that needed to be kept hidden from the authorities.'

'Fool!' said Markham, glaring at Draycott. 'Whether he's genuine or not, we cannot take the risk after you allowed your mouth to run away with itself. We clearly need to confine him until we're ready to head south, and preferably for a lot longer than that.'

'You are both mistaken,' Edward insisted, then turned as he became aware of stealthy movement behind him. Howard de Vere stood only feet away from him with a drawn sword.

'I may have to live with this on my conscience,' said Markham, 'but the prize is too great for unnecessary risks. You will be confined below ground until we have departed from here in a few days' time. But even then you will not be released, because one of the many facilities that comes with a house of this age is a cellar where men may be imprisoned until they die of thirst or starvation. Either that or they go mad. It is regrettable, but I have no choice. Go with Master de Vere, and be advised that he would like nothing better than to run you through if you resist.'

Edward was escorted into another wing of the house that he had not previously encountered, and which he took to be some sort of north wing. It appeared older than the rest of the house, and it had a flagstone floor. Two of de Vere's companions lifted one of the flags, and Edward was ordered down a short flight of narrow stairs into a cavity that lay beneath it.

It was bad enough that there was barely enough room for Edward to stretch out to his full six feet inside the narrow space beneath the stone, which resembled a saint's sarcophagus. But it was much worse when the slab was hammered back into place above his head, and he was plunged into total darkness.

14

Barely able to move his limbs, Edward cursed his own stupidity, then allowed himself to cry tears of impotence and fear as he contemplated the miserable end that awaited him.

He thought of Elizabeth, who would soon become a widow with four fatherless children, the last of which he would never hold. How long before it became known what had happened to him? It was possible that no-one would ever learn of his fate. If Markham and his fellow conspirators succeeded in toppling James from the throne and introducing their own monarch, would they ever reveal what they had done with the man who had sought to thwart their plans? And if they failed, and were sent to Tower Hill for the ritual hanging, drawing and quartering that awaited all unsuccessful traitors, would their secret die with them?

He had no way of measuring the passage of time, and no hope of rescue, so he decided to resign himself to his fate and make his peace with God. He'd turned his back on the Church many years ago, sickened by the weaknesses of so-called men of God and the wicked venality of the Church of Rome. But somehow he'd clung to a belief that there was salvation after death, a higher world in which one day he might embrace Elizabeth once again, and watch over his children. There he would be reunited with his birth mother, and perhaps finally meet his father — the priest who had broken his vows.

He felt himself being surrounded by a swirling mist as his grip on reality weakened, and he began to fall asleep. When he opened his eyes, there appeared to be a dim light above his head, and through it he could just make out the faint image of his late mother as he remembered her, smiling down at him. She turned her head to one side, and another faint circle of light revealed a handsome man with finely cut features surmounted by a monk's tonsure. Edward wondered silently if the man might be his father, and as if reading his thoughts his mother nodded, and seemed to take the man's hand. Then, as the light grew brighter, they each reached out with their spare hands to pull him into Heaven with them. He smiled lovingly and nodded his willingness to go, then suddenly the light became unbearably bright. He heard a voice.

'Thank God you're still alive!' said Robbie Bishop as he threw down the iron bar with which he'd succeeded in prising up the stone slab. He reached out to pull Edward free of his intended tomb.

'How long was I down there?' Edward asked hoarsely as he gasped in the sweetest fresh air he could ever remember, then recoiled from the stench of his soiled clothing.

'Three days, I reckon,' Robbie replied, 'though I don't rightly know when they put you down there.'

'The same day that you arrived in the camp,' Edward told him.

'You're lucky to still be alive.'

'How on earth did you find me, and how did you manage to avoid a similar fate?' Edward asked as he walked a few steps back and forth, regaining the use of his cramped limbs.

'I nearly didn't. When that bloke Draycott come back from Ollerton without you, I had a feeling summat wasn't right, so I walked over to the horse. Then when Draycott said that I was a spy, and ordered some men to come and tie me up, I jumped on the horse and got out of there. Then I hid in some trees, wondering where you might've got to, 'til I saw them all riding this way, and followed them.'

'So they've all left?' Edward asked, horrified. 'How long ago was that?'

'Two days ago, but I wasn't sure whether to follow them or come looking for you. I hope I've done the right thing?'

'What do *you* think?' Edward laughed and was then overtaken by a fit of coughing. 'Anyway,' he added as he regained control of his breathing, 'we need to set off after them, or perhaps alert the authorities. I need time to think things through carefully, since I made a right mess of things when I just followed my instinct. Thanks to you I lived to tell the tale, but now I need some fresh clothes, and some food and drink.'

'I already saw to that,' Robbie told him, 'in the hope that I'd find you alive.'

'I knew it was a wise move to appoint you as a constable,' said Edward as he put an arm over Robbie's shoulder. 'I know I don't smell too good, but I should be able to walk on my own after I've eaten something.'

On the slow walk out of the north wing, and then through the entrance hall onto the service stairs that led down to the kitchen, Robbie told the rest of his story. Once satisfied that there would probably be no resistance offered after the large group of men had left Ollerton Hall, and suspecting that Edward had been confined somewhere inside it, Robbie had found the steward, grabbed him by the throat and held him up against a wall until he revealed what had befallen Edward. The terrified steward had then brought Robbie tools and shown him the stone under which Edward had been incarcerated.

Condor had also confessed that Edward had been without food and drink for the previous three days. Therefore, while waiting for the tools to be brought to him, Robbie had gone into the kitchen and ordered the woman seemingly in charge to make up some beef broth. Then he'd been the one to prise up the lid of Edward's intended tomb, while Condor scurried off somewhere to hide.

By the time they reached the kitchen Edward was walking normally. He removed his hand from Robbie's shoulder as he waved in acknowledgement of the cheery welcome he received from the woman there, who introduced herself as Lily.

'Is it right, what this strapping young man said — that you were locked up by the master?' she asked, handing him a mug of water, which Edward downed in one go.

He nodded. 'I'm afraid so, but Robbie here was able to find out where they'd put me, and dug me out. I hope you won't be in trouble for feeding me.'

'Nowt to worry about there,' Lily muttered, 'since we've all been told we don't work here anymore. The master took off with all the blokes that have been hanging around him these past few weeks, and good riddance as far as that goes. Then he told us we'd all been dismissed, so we got drunk on what was left of his wine and had a big party. There's food enough left in here for a week or more, so we'll just sit tight until that runs out, then the good Lord knows what'll happen to us. But sit yourself down while I ladle out some of this beef broth that your friend ordered. It's a pleasure to be of service, seeing as how it was you who brought that lovely woman Rose in here. She made sure we were treated better. The least I can do is put some strength back in you, so sit down and get stuck in. There's plenty, and your friend there can help himself to some of that leftover pork on the side. It's only a day or so old, and there's fresh bread from this morning and all.'

After Edward and Robbie had eaten as much as they could, and Edward felt the energy flowing back into his muscles, he asked Lily where Steward Condor might be hiding. 'I'm going to need a change of clothes before we set off,' he explained.

'Last I saw of him, he was scurrying into the stables, looking like a rabbit being chased by a ferret,' Lily said with a chuckle.

'Leave him to me,' said Robbie, grinning sadistically as he rose and left the kitchen. He returned a few minutes later with fresh hose, a woollen jerkin and a crumpled undershirt. 'I got another horse as well,' he told Edward. 'The steward sends his compliments, and when would you like him to lick your boots by way of an apology?'

'There's no call for that,' Edward laughed as he peeled off his soiled clothing and changed into the fresh garments, earning a few admiring glances from several of the kitchen maids. 'However,' he announced once he was dressed, 'we must head off without delay.'

'Together?' asked Robbie. 'Don't you want me to ride to Ashby and tell that lord that lives there that there's a mob of armed men heading down to London who mean the king no good? Then you can set off after them, like you planned.'

'I *had* hoped to be one of their number,' Edward reflected, 'but that option is no longer open. They have several days' start on us, and may well reach London before we can catch up with them. I take it that they were all on horseback?'

'Most of them,' said Robbie, 'but the ones from Sherwood were being carried in wagons, so that'll slow them down a bit, I reckon. You should be able to overtake them, if you ride hard on that lively horse of yours.'

'Then what?' Edward asked. 'They obviously know me, and the fact that I was seeking to expose them. If I show my face anywhere near them, they'll simply kill me. They fondly imagine that they already have, remember, so that gives us the advantage.'

'What are you suggesting?' Robbie asked.

'We both ride hard south to Ashby,' Edward told him. 'There I can alert the earl; he can dispatch a messenger south to Cecil, who I imagine is constantly in attendance on the king.'

'Then we've done our job, and can go back to Nottingham?'

'Not just yet, I'm afraid. I'll require you to remain in Ashby to guard three women and four children, with another two on the way. Then, and only then, will I head off south.'

'You're going to take on that lot of murderers on your own?' Robbie asked.

'No, I think I've pushed my luck too far in that direction already. I'm going after Markham and his rogues, but not alone.'

'Daddy!' Robert shouted joyfully as he leapt from the front steps of the dower house, on which Rose was teaching the four children how to weave baskets from straw. Alerted by the shout, Francis appeared in the doorway, then came quickly down the steps to shake hands with his old friend.

'You're still in time for the births,' he told Edward. 'Kitty will finally be taking to her childbed sometime this week, according to Rose, while Elizabeth's only a week or so behind her. So, assuming that all you have left to do is alert the earl to the departure of those with evil intent, then you may remain in time for both events.'

'It's only an estimate, mind,' Rose warned them as she rose from where she had been seated. 'You can never be certain of these things, and it's some years since I attended a lying-in. But come in, Edward, and let me find some food for you and your friend. To judge by the height of the sun, it's high time I began the preparations for dinner anyway.'

They ducked into the shade of the short entrance hall, then walked the five paces into the room at the rear that served as an all-purpose living chamber. There Elizabeth and Kitty sat in comfortable chairs with their feet on footstools, their stomachs protruding before them. Elizabeth looked Edward up and down, then asked sarcastically, 'Do I know you?'

'You did once,' he said with a grin, 'which is how you finished up in this condition. Rose tells me you will soon be relieved.'

'And not a moment too soon! Now come, lean down and kiss me, for the prospect of rising to my feet is a daunting one. You may also give me your latest excuse for leaving almost as soon as you arrive.'

Edward did as instructed, and the long, lingering kiss, being well overdue, was all the sweeter for them both. But his conscience drove an arrow through his heart as he contemplated telling her that he would almost certainly need to depart long before she went into the final stages of childbirth.

'Francis and Elizabeth will remember Robbie Bishop, of course, but for different reasons,' he told the company. 'Francis knows him as a town constable, while Elizabeth will recall that he stoutly defended our house in town while I set about proving Francis's innocence of murder. I now know him as the man to whom I owe my life, after Sir Griffin Markham threw me into a coffin under the floor of the north wing of his house. Robbie was able to free me once my gaoler took off with his mob of cut-throats in order to kidnap the king.'

'They have already left?' Francis asked anxiously.

Edward nodded. 'Indeed they have, and we must lose no time in alerting those who guard His Majesty, then riding south in order to unmask those who are engaged in the plot.'

'I knew it!' Elizabeth muttered. She looked across at Kitty and added, 'At least yours stays at home for long enough to fulfil his responsibilities as a husband and father.'

'I cannot even remain at home to eat my dinner,' Edward announced as he turned to leave. 'I must speak to the Earl of Huntingdon without delay. At least he will recognise the peril that currently threatens the nation, even if my wife cannot see beyond the bulge in her gown.'

An hour later Sir George was listening to what Edward was able to relate to him of recent events.

'We may be too late, I fear,' he said. 'Even were I to despatch a messenger this very day, he would be unlikely to be able to alert Cecil in time for him to double the guard around the king.'

'I have given that difficulty considerable thought,' Edward told him solemnly, 'and my proposal is that I ride south without breaking stride except to change horses, and head them off in person. I know them by sight, I know the nature of their plan, and I believe I may be able to turn at least some of their following from the purpose of which many remain unaware. Some of them believe that they are travelling to court merely in order to present a petition to His Majesty, and that the successful outcome may be the relief of their own personal suffering. Others have been deceived into the belief that they are about to embark on an overseas venture that will bring them great personal riches. When they learn how callously they have been duped, I have hopes that they will turn aside, and perhaps even turn *against* their deceivers.'

'It is perhaps the best action to take,' the earl agreed, 'and indeed it may be the only *possible* action. But one man alone?'

'There will be two of us,' Edward assured him.

Sir George laughed. 'That reminds me of a jest I once heard regarding how the entire might of the Roman army was defeated by two lone Scotsmen, but no matter. It is a desperate measure, but perhaps the only one left to us. I will despatch my messenger anyway, but what else can I do to further your madcap scheme?'

'You can advise me where I might catch up with Cecil and the king.'

'I can tell you only what I know, and that knowledge is more than a week old. But last I heard, His Majesty was still residing with Cecil at Theobalds House. He delays his entry into London due to the ongoing presence therein of the pestilence, and it is rumoured that his coronation will also be delayed until a more propitious time. If you ride hard, as you propose, you might reach Theobalds within three days. Do you know its location?'

Edward looked perplexed, so the earl continued.

'Theobalds House lies in Hertfordshire, hard by the village of Waltham Cross. Your most direct route would be by way of Leicester, Northampton and St Albans. I can supply you with horses, and the coin with which to pay for those things you will need on your journey.'

'I thank you, but all that I ask is that you see to the welfare of those I shall be leaving behind in the dower house,' Edward replied as he rose to leave. 'They are most precious to me.'

'I understand,' the earl nodded, 'and rest assured that they will be well guarded and provided for. Now I can only wish you Godspeed.'

'Pray that God continues to shower His mercy and blessings upon me,' Edward muttered as he bowed, turned and left hurriedly.

He found Francis waiting for him as he dismounted outside the dower house.

'You have spoken with the earl?' Francis asked.

'I have,' said Edward, 'and I must leave without delay.'

'Earlier, when speaking of your intended journey south, you said "we",' Francis reminded him. 'I am no longer content simply to guard women and children. You can safely entrust that task to young Robbie. I wish to accompany you.'

Edward grinned. 'What makes you think that I did not intend for that to happen? But there is a heavy price you must pay first.'

'What might that be?' Francis asked.

Edward nodded towards the open door to the dower house. 'You must go back in there and explain matters to our wives.'

15

'My arse feels like someone lit a bonfire under it,' Francis complained bitterly between laboured breaths as they clattered through the second day, on their third mounts. They'd left Ashby early on the previous day and had cleared Leicester by nightfall. They were now approaching a village on the rutted track that they hoped would take them to Northampton.

'It's my throat that's on fire,' Edward croaked. 'If the village we are approaching possesses an inn with a stables, then let's bide there for a while. I suspect that my mount has few miles left in her anyway.'

The proprietor of the Welford Arms was more than happy to welcome two hungry, thirsty travellers who appeared to be men of substance. Once he'd brought them large pots of small beer and a generous platter of bread and cheese, Edward persuaded Francis to stop walking up and down like a duck in order to bring the feeling back into his thighs, and sit down beside him on the bench outside the alehouse.

'How much further must we ride?' Francis asked grumpily.

Edward shrugged. 'Since I have never travelled this road before, I have no idea. I only know where we departed from, and where we are headed, which is a township called Waltham Cross. It is close by the home of Cecil, a place called Theobalds House, where it is believed that the king is in residence. The next town of any substance that we are headed for is called Northampton, and from there we must strike across to a place called St Albans. Once there we shall be within a good day's ride of Waltham Cross, or so I was advised by the earl, who calculated that we would be at least three days on the road.'

Francis groaned and banged his half empty ale pot down onto the rough surface of the bench at which they were seated. 'God help us,' he muttered, 'and all because of some parboiled notion that there is a plot to kidnap the king.'

'I am relying on what your sister-in-law overheard when she hid from view in the main hall of Ollerton Hall,' said Edward. 'It was clear from what she heard that Markham is in league with others, some as highly placed as Sir Walter Raleigh, a court favourite of Elizabeth's, although from what Sir George told me he has fallen from grace of late.'

'And do you have names for the other conspirators?' Francis challenged him as he claimed the last piece of cheese.

'Only the names that Rose was able to supply,' Edward replied as he made a point of reaching out for the greater half of the remaining manchet loaf. 'She mentioned two brothers by the name of "Brooke", although the earl is of the opinion that Cecil may not proceed against them on account of the fact that he was married to their sister, although she is dead now.'

'So you have the so-called conspiracy of one man, who for all you know may be bereft of his wits — as foolhardy and arrogant as Essex when he thought he could raise an army against the late queen,' Francis summarised in a surly tone. 'Have you come up with a plan for when we finally catch up with this band of adventurers, assuming that we do?'

Edward frowned. 'I have obviously given the matter some thought while we have been on the road. I was advised by Robbie, who saw them leave Ollerton, that while the gentlemen who have been living easily as Markham's dissolute guests were all on horseback, the peasants I've been attempting to train were crammed into wagons. They will obviously have travelled more slowly than those on horseback, which means two things. The first is that those we are pursuing will not be a united body when we catch up with them. The second point, which we may use to our advantage, is that the peasant contingent may well be as discontented with their lot as you appear to be at present. I have hopes that I can divert them from their mission.'

'Perhaps,' Francis replied sarcastically, 'in order to test your recently acquired power to perform miracles, we should search out some nearby stream, whose waters you may command to flow backwards?'

'You are either with me, or against me,' Edward replied sharply as his tolerance dwindled. 'If it's the latter, leave me to go on alone. Go back to your apple orchard, your widow and your easy life, and leave me to save the nation from ruin.'

'I dare not return to Ashby alone,' Francis admitted, 'for fear of Elizabeth's wrath.'

'And she is not even *your* wife,' Edward said with a chuckle. 'Get off your arse, Francis, and at least provide me with someone to complain to as the road ahead proves endless.'

'Never let it be said that Barton failed Mountsorrel, however mad his scheme,' Francis muttered with reluctance. 'Let us see if the mountebank who took our coin in exchange for cheese that tasted like yesterday's curds can produce two horses, each with four legs.'

Freshly horsed, the remainder of their day was taken up by the ride through Northampton. They reached an uneven track that they were assured by a ragged boy leaning on an alehouse post would take them to St Albans. As night began to fall, Francis suggested that they bed down by the side of the road, but Edward shook his head.

'We know not how far away St Albans is. That last milestone claimed it was thirty miles, but I have known such markers to be wrong. So we must press ahead, and by daylight we may be at some place where we can make enquiry regarding the road to Waltham Cross. *Then* we might consider a late breakfast.'

'Or a Last Supper,' Francis suggested drily.

St Albans was busy the following morning as they walked their tired mounts slowly through what looked like a marketplace. Edward nodded towards the jettied building whose hanging sign declared it to be The Tudor Rose.

'Therein lies our next brief rest. But we need fresh horses, and perhaps a change of hose. We may even gain intelligence of the whereabouts of those we have been following.'

Francis was almost nodding off, his head wobbling perilously close to the bench in front of the recently lit fire as the landlord laid a platter of pork down before them. A lad followed behind with a loaf of bread, and a girl of little more than twelve filled their pots with indifferent ale.

'Your horses are outside, when you need them,' their host told them, 'though by the looks of you both, and meaning no disrespect, you might best be advised to stay here until tomorrow. I've got a nice clean chamber above here that's got two fine new bolsters in it, and then you can set out on your travels fully refreshed. I take it you're headed for London?'

'Not while the plague remains there,' Edward told him. 'As a matter of fact, we're bound for Waltham Cross, there to pay our respects to the new king. We're advised he may be in residence at the country home of Sir Robert Cecil — a place called Theobalds House?'

'They reckon he's been made Viscount Cranborne recently,' the innkeeper replied, 'on account of the fact that the king's been staying at his big house for weeks now. But there are that

151

many who've passed through here on the way to give their loyal greetings, like you gentlemen, that you'll likely find that there are no rooms left in any of the local alehouses. It's only a full day's ride from here, down the road that goes through Brookmans Park, so why not stay here instead?'

'You look better mannered than the last lot, anyroad,' the youth told them with a surly expression.

The landlord turned to glare at him, before turning back to his guests with an apology. 'My boy Ned's new to the business, and he doesn't appreciate that the proper gentry, like those folks were, like to enjoy themselves from time to time. They got a bit merry, that's all. Like you, they were off to see the king, so no wonder they were all excited. The man they were with was a right gent, with a title and all.'

'Not Sir Griffin Markham, by any chance?' Edward asked.

'Sounds about right,' the landlord agreed. 'There were a few others with him, and we couldn't provide rooms for them all, so some of them had to go down the street to The Griffin. That's how I remember the gent's name, see?'

'And the ones with him were all gentry, you say?' Edward persisted. 'You didn't by any chance see a larger group, more poorly attired, and travelling in wagons?'

'That was yesterday,' the landlord told them. 'The gents who stayed here went off three days ago, but they said to look out for a collection of wagons coming south behind them, and that the folks in them might need food and drink. As it happens, only one of them did, and he stayed here. Then he left without paying, so if you catch up with him, you might tell the miserly bastard that the constable's been informed.'

'I'd be delighted to oblige,' Edward said, 'if you can confirm that his name was Draycott.'

'That wasn't the name he gave me,' the landlord grumbled. 'He said his name was Sherwood, and he was leading a group of men from the estate of that Markham bloke who'd stayed here two nights previously. Maybe *he'll* have the good grace to pay me what I'm due, him being such a gent.'

'But you saw the group that was following behind their master, did you?' Edward prompted.

The landlord nodded. 'There must've been thirty or so of them, riding in three wagons. They were asking where they might set up camp for the night, so I sent them out Napsbury way, where there are lots of fields and the like.'

'And this was, what, yesterday, you said?' Edward asked. The landlord confirmed this. Edward told the landlord that they would indeed be happy to stay the night, but that they would be leaving before daybreak the following morning.

'We're only a day behind them,' Francis reminded Edward once the landlord had waddled back to the kitchen. 'Why don't we just push on and surprise them as night is falling?'

'I wasn't planning a full-scale charge, two against thirty,' said Edward, 'even though I've no idea if they're armed. If they've been given swords, then they're more danger to themselves than any attacker. But more to the point, we have no idea where they might be found.'

'Didn't our host tell us?' Francis asked.

Edward shook his head. 'He only told us where they were likely to have been *last* night. They may still be at that Napsbury place, but they've almost certainly pushed on. I propose that we take this opportunity to refresh ourselves, get a full night's sleep, then ride hard after them and catch them as they're in the process of setting up camp wherever they may be tomorrow.'

The next morning, there were only a handful of stallholders setting out their wares in the marketplace as Edward and Francis rode out of the township, and onto the road that would take them to Waltham Cross.

As the sun rose to a position directly above their heads, they came up behind a cloud of dust, through which they could see the faint outline of a wagon that appeared to be the last one in a line of perhaps three or four.

'Hang back,' Edward instructed Francis as he pulled on his own horse's reins, 'and let them guide us to their next camp. It wants the best part of another day before they reach Theobalds House. No doubt they'll be intending to make permanent camp either here or slightly closer to the place, leaving Draycott to advise Markham that he has the men ready. We'll give them time to settle in and let their guard down, then I'll pay them a visit.'

'While I go in search of acorns for our supper?' Francis asked with heavy sarcasm. 'Wherever you go, I go.'

'They don't know you,' Edward argued.

'Some of them will, if they're among those we've thrown out of the town in recent weeks. But no matter, because you'll no doubt introduce me, so that they know who's about to cut their balls off.'

'England can give grateful thanks that it never had need of your services as an ambassador,' said Edward. 'But for the time being, we dismount.'

154

16

'I could never claim that life after I became associated with Edward Mountsorrel lacked excitement,' Francis muttered as he wiped the grass off his hose. They were sitting at the side of the track that, according to the marker stone against which Edward was resting his back, would lead them to Waltham Cross in a further four miles.

'Surely, it's been more of a friendship than an "association"?' Edward replied.

Francis turned to regard him wryly. 'Since I've known you, I've been thrown into a dungeon in the rocks below Nottingham Castle, falsely accused of murder, forced to attend a gallows site reputed to be haunted by the souls of the dead, and now — *this*,' Francis went on. 'If that's friendship, then I'd have fared better as your bitter enemy.'

'You can't blame me for the accusation that you murdered the Widow Timberlake,' Edward protested, 'given that you'd been joyously cavorting with her before the pair of you were slipped drugged wine. As for getting yourself locked up beneath the castle, I was half a nation away at the time, rescuing prostitutes on their way to Scotland in Cecil's retinue. You decided to investigate those dungeons by yourself. And you *did* insist on accompanying me down here to intercept those intent on kidnapping the king.'

'I did not know then that you would be proposing to confront thirty trained and armed men with a polite request that they lay down their swords and return to Nottingham.'

'First of all, they are hardly "trained",' Edward countered. 'I can vouch for that myself, since I attempted to train them.

They are desperate men whose families face starvation, and they only fell in with Draycott because he promised them something better. As for weapons, if they've been supplied with any at all, then they are at greater risk of maiming themselves with them than they are of inflicting any injury on an enemy. That said, no doubt that posturing fool de Vere was assigned to their training after Draycott and Markham thought that I'd been consigned to death, so perhaps they've been taught how to terrify the enemy with arrogant boasts.'

'The fact remains,' Francis persisted, 'that having travelled for the best part of a week down rutted tracks in rickety wagons, in the belief that His Majesty will listen sympathetically to their pleas for charity, they are hardly likely to be persuaded to return to Sherwood just a few miles from their destination.'

'That remains to be seen,' Edward insisted. 'But if you have any better plan, then this might be a good time to reveal it, while they're resting ahead of the final leg of their pilgrimage.'

They'd finally found what was almost certainly the last camp of the Sherwood component of Markham's intended insurrection army. A group of four wagons and tired-looking horses had been arranged around crude canvas shelters that looked incapable of withstanding even a moderate wind. Several fires had been lit, and it looked, from a distance, as if men had been dispatched into adjacent woodland in search of small game that might constitute their next meal. They were less than half a mile distant, in a field to the left of the track down which Edward and Francis had been cautiously walking their horses, when they caught sight of the group, dismounted, and seated themselves behind a hedge.

'So when do you intend to attempt this miracle of oratory?' Francis demanded, and Edward rose to his feet in silent reply.

Francis groaned and followed his example, then asked, 'Do we take the horses, in case they possess greater powers of persuasion?'

'Perhaps it's best that we do,' Edward replied nervously, 'since it will make our escape much speedier if your gloomy prediction becomes reality, and they prefer the certainty of armed rebellion to the uncertainty of their miserable lives at present.'

As Francis continued to mutter against the insanity of what they were about to do, they trotted off the track and into the field. Edward noted that the inexperienced rebels hadn't even set a guard against intruders. He and Francis were just yards away from the circle camp when one of the men happened to look up from his attempts to strike flame into recently gathered brushwood and gave a hoarse shout.

'It's Master Mountsorrel! They said he was dead, but here's his ghost!'

'I would indeed be dead, had it been left to your verminous so-called leader,' Edward replied in loud, confident tones, 'but I'm here to ensure that none of you meet a similar fate.'

'And how's that, then?' another man called out as he emerged from behind the cover of a wagon, waving a sword.

Edward looked at the sword and laughed. 'Have you achieved anything with that blade other than cutting yourself, Blidworth? And in my absence, did that slack-mouthed popinjay de Vere convince you all that you'd become soldiers?'

'He most certainly did,' announced the man who appeared from behind one of the other wagons, a sword held firmly in his hand. Edward pulled a face and turned to speak to Francis.

'Allow me to introduce the most boastful pig's bladder in the service of Sir Griffin Markham. That least known, and least able, traitor to the English Crown, Howard de Vere, who once deserted the service of the Earl of Essex. Not content with that, he now hopes to inflate his fortunes as well as his opinion of himself by leading a body of ill-trained and ill-disciplined clods in a futile attempt to prevent James of Scotland from becoming King of England.'

De Vere's mouth twisted in a sneer as he advanced slowly towards Edward with his sword still extended. 'You may not have died in Ollerton Hall, you yaldson, but I'm about to remedy that. If your companion would care to stand back politely, I'll endeavour not to get your blood on his tunic.'

'My companion is the bailiff of Nottinghamshire,' Edward replied defiantly, 'and one of his many talents is extracting swords from braggarts who challenged the wrong adversary, so his presence here will be fortuitous.'

'That's right,' called out one of those who had gathered on the fringes of what promised to be an interesting contest, 'that bloke really *is* the county bailiff — he threw me back in a wagon one time when we were caught on our way into Nottingham.'

'Shut your mouth!' commanded another voice from inside the ring of wagons, as Draycott appeared from nowhere, an evil smirk on his face. He stood a few feet behind de Vere, nodding with approval. 'Finish him off, Howard, then we can all have something to eat.'

'It will be my pleasure,' de Vere snarled as he continued walking slowly towards Edward, his sword still raised to waist height.

'What was that about opposing the king?' another voice asked from among the spectators.

Draycott turned towards him with an angry glare. 'You'll find out soon enough — now shut your mouth, and let's see some *real* swordplay.'

Edward decided that it was time to draw his own blade, given that de Vere was now only ten feet away. He withdrew it from the scabbard and held it out at waist height, in the traditional opening stance for a swordfight.

'So, you want to play, do you?' de Vere asked.

Edward replied with a harsh laugh. 'Well, I'm hardly likely to stand here and let you run me through, am I?'

With an angry shout of challenge, de Vere rushed at Edward, his blade extended. Edward parried the first thrust with a downward slash of his own blade, then leapt back a few paces. De Vere came back at him with a jabbing thrust, but Edward jinked to one side and caught his opponent's right arm with a sweeping cut of his own that ripped a wide slash in de Vere's tunic. Blood oozed through as he backed away, nursing the wound. The injury had been to his sword arm, which was now hanging limply.

Edward shouted across the six feet or so that now separated them. 'I will take your formal surrender now, if you wish to see to that somewhat inconvenient flesh wound.'

'Yield, Howard,' Draycott ordered him, 'and it may be that we can find some way to bind the wound before we challenge the king tomorrow.'

'How do you mean, challenge the king?' one of Draycott's party asked. 'You said we were just giving him a petition.'

'He told you that, did he?' said Francis. 'Well, Bailiff Mountsorrel here can give the lie to that. You've been recruited to kidnap the king at the very least, and perhaps even put him to death. Allow me to describe in detail the manner of the death that awaits traitors.'

'All in good time,' Edward replied. 'The first matter to be clarified is whether or not Master de Vere wishes to continue the fight with his sword in his only remaining hand, which is not the one he favours.'

'I'm not yielding to some peasant like you,' de Vere muttered.

Draycott stepped out from behind him and placed a restraining hand on his limp arm. 'You are. There are enough men here to deal with Bailiff Mountsorrel and his talking saddle pony. So set to it, men — there's a pound for the man who finally shuts his mouth.'

'De Vere couldn't kill me, so what makes you think that *they* can?' Edward scoffed.

'And they'll also be dealing with me,' Francis added as he drew his sword. 'Killing two bailiffs will result in a *very* slow hanging for treason, with possibly a disembowelling to follow, just before you choke your last. So form a polite line for the hangman.'

'We didn't agree to treason,' a man towards the rear of the awestricken group called out, to several shouts of support from those around him. 'Ain't it right that we're just going to talk to the king about how folks are suffering, and the need to find work for us, so that we can provide for our families?'

'That was never the plan,' Edward told them. 'You've all been misled by the man you thought was your friend. The man who dined almost daily in the big house in Ollerton, taking orders from the *real* instigator of what's being planned when you all proceed to Theobalds House, four miles further down the road. The king is residing there with Secretary of State Cecil, and you can rest assured that none of you will be allowed within smelling distance of James of Scotland. The only purpose you're intended to serve is to look like some sort of armed band, giving the impression that Markham and his fellow traitors have a following. But you still have time to withdraw and go back to your camp in Sherwood, and I will personally ensure that Secretary Cecil acknowledges that you were duped. It may even be that he can prevail upon the king to give you alms, and perhaps some hope of future work in the royal forest that most of you have lived in or around for most of your lives.'

'Don't listen to that fool!' Draycott called out. 'He's been spying on you all since the first day he set foot in the camp, pretending that he'd been dismissed from his office. If he could lie about that, then he can lie about why we're off to see the king. Now set about the pair of them, and let's have done with this nonsense!'

Nobody moved. Instead, the Sherwood men began muttering among themselves, shaking their heads and looking confused. Edward was encouraged to make a further offer that he had no authorisation to issue, but which would be likely to settle the matter.

'Before I left my duties in the town, at the personal request of Secretary Cecil, who'd received word of a plan to kidnap the king, the sheriffs who employ me were about to open an almshouse where that Hospitaller sanctuary used to be, at the far end of Backside. It will provide food, shelter and regular employment for men such as yourselves, along with your families. If you disperse now and go about your lawful return to Sherwood, I'll see to it that you are all afforded shelter in there, as the first to be taken in. It has to be a better prospect that petitioning the king, surely? There are thousands like you, up and down the realm, so why should he give favourable regard to just a few like yourselves? You weren't going to be offered the chance to petition him anyway, and most of you would have perished on the blades of royal guards. So which is it to be?'

'Don't listen to that stupid mongrel!' Draycott yelled, as at least half the assembled group that he'd brought all the way from Sherwood began talking loudly and angrily among themselves. 'He's just been sent by those who rule the country to talk you out of presenting your petition!' Draycott added desperately.

One of the men turned to challenge him. 'You keep going on about that petition, but we ain't seen it yet. So where is it?'

'Yeah!' shouted another man. 'Show us your petition!'

'He doesn't have one!' Edward shouted back in response. 'There never was one, and you've all been brought here to look like an army, which you're not. If you were to go with him into that big house down the road, you'd all be arrested, imprisoned, and then hanged for treason. Your best action now is just to go home.'

'And quickly!' Francis added as he saw a column of mounted soldiers trotting into the field, all of them sporting royal-looking livery. 'If you move now, they can't catch all of you.'

Draycott's pretend army scattered in all directions, but predominantly further into the field, then across ditches and clean through hedgerows into the adjoining woodland. Draycott decided to join them, despite a stern admonition from Francis to remain where he was. Then de Vere gave an angry roar and leapt towards Edward, his sword in his undamaged hand.

'Give me one good reason why I shouldn't kill you!' he said to Edward, who stepped back a few paces and held his own sword out in front of him.

'I can give you three. First of all, I'm a better swordsman than you. Secondly, you're reduced to fighting with the wrong arm. And thirdly, my wife wouldn't permit it.'

His wry response had the desired effect. Forgetting every rule of self-discipline taught to swordsmen, de Vere ran at Edward with a howl of desperation, his weapon high above his head. This time Edward felt no compunction to be merciful. As his blade slid into de Vere's upper torso with a sickening squelch, his would-be attacker gave a terrible scream. His knees buckled, and he slid to the ground, leaving Edward with the simple task of placing one foot on de Vere's prone form, then pulling his blade out of the gaping wound.

'That's dealt with him,' Edward gasped as he regained his breath and saw Francis by his side.

'Very good,' Francis replied as he turned and nodded behind them. 'Now perhaps you'd care to deal with *them*.'

Edward turned and became aware of the column of liveried soldiers who were in the process of dismounting, and the line of wagons that was entering the field from the track that led to Waltham Cross. An older man walked towards where Edward and Francis stood waiting, his sword drawn and his stern face denoting his authority as he glared at Edward.

'I'm Captain Conway of the Westminster Guard, and you're being taken up for murder.'

'What, for killing *him*?' Edward protested as he nodded towards de Vere's body. 'If ever a man deserved to be exterminated like a rat, it was Howard de Vere. And you may have noticed that he drew his weapon on me first, so that my actions were in my own defence.'

'I was too busy watching your companions making a run for it,' Conway replied.

Edward laughed. 'That lot? They were the ones I was sent to head off, before they reached Theobalds House.'

'Then why are you dressed like the rest of them?' Conway asked.

'We've been on the road for three days, following them,' Edward explained in a tone bordering on exasperation. 'I'm Edward Mountsorrel, bailiff to the Sheriff of Nottingham.'

Conway shook his head. 'The man you just killed looked more like a bailiff than you do, so put your arms behind you for binding, then get into that wagon that's being brought up for your transport to the nearest dungeon.'

'If that's inside Theobalds House, then all well and good,' said Edward. 'But be sure to mention my name to Sir Robert Cecil.'

'I suppose you're about to claim to be a friend of his?'

'No — I was working for him.'

'One minute you claim to be working for the Sheriff of Nottingham, then it's Viscount Cranborne. Just get in the wagon,' Conway ordered Edward as his hands were roped behind his back.

'He really is the Bailiff of Nottingham,' Francis insisted.

Conway turned to him. 'And who might you be?'

'Bailiff to the Sheriff of Nottinghamshire.'

'Of course you are. And I'm the Countess of Hereford. Just get in the wagon along with your fellow traitor.'

'Like I said,' Francis muttered as the wagoner flicked the reins and the wagon jerked into motion, with Edward and Francis rolling in the back, 'it's never lacking in excitement, working with Edward Mountsorrel.'

17

'I can only offer you both my profuse apologies for the manner of your arrival here,' Cecil said in the humblest tone that either Edward or Francis had ever heard him employ. 'My only excuse is that I had no idea you had been pursuing that peasant rabble.'

'Did the Earl of Huntingdon not advise you that such was his instruction to me?' Edward asked grumpily.

Cecil shook his head. 'Unfortunately he did not. My only knowledge of their imminent arrival was from Sir Griffin Markham, and he did not, shall we say, reveal that information voluntarily. You no doubt heard his vain calls for his immediate release from the cell adjoining yours?'

'We did, but they sounded more like the pleas of a man about to undergo torture,' Francis replied with a shudder.

'As I say, he was not a willing provider of information — to begin with, anyway,' said Cecil. 'But have some more of this excellent Burgundy, and put those unfortunate memories to flight.'

They were seated in Cecil's private suite of rooms inside Theobalds House, where an array of large windows offered a view of verdant lawns sweeping down to a summer house. The room was heavily and expensively panelled with cedar, and there was a generous fireplace that looked capable of consuming an entire forest in one day. Since they were now in the middle of a warm summer the fireplace was not in use, and the irons had been polished to a shine. It was a stark contrast to the last chamber they had occupied in the house, from which they'd been hastily extracted once Captain Conway had inadvertently mentioned that the only prisoners they'd managed to acquire a few miles to the north were insisting that their names were Mountsorrel and Barton, and that they were both bailiffs.

'So Markham revealed that he had a small force of badly trained men at arms waiting to lay siege to this place?' Francis asked.

Cecil twitched with irritation. 'This *place*, as you call it, was commissioned by my late father, in the finest red brick to be had anywhere in England, and was regularly visited by Queen Elizabeth. It is now playing host to James of Scotland, shortly to become James of England *and* Scotland, since it is deemed to be the finest house outside London in which our new monarch can receive the loyal pledges of his Privy Council, of which, of course, I am the principal member.'

'What made you suspicious of Markham in the first place?' Edward asked in the hope of preventing Francis putting his other undiplomatic foot in his mouth.

'As you know from our previous meeting, I was made aware of his intrigue regarding a certain lady in Derbyshire by those remaining Catholics who wish to prevent any precipitate action by hotheads whose misguided faith urges them to excess in all things. Markham was thought at that time to be in league with others, and thanks to Master Mountsorrel here we now know that two of these are the brothers Brooke.' He caught the anxious look in Edward's eyes and smiled reassuringly. 'I am aware that you know of my former family relationship with those two gentlemen, and I may confide that the only time my late wife and I found ourselves at odds was in connection with her misguided affection for her two brothers. They were idle wasters then, as they are now, and they will no doubt remain so until their lives are strangled from them on Tower Hill.'

'Markham has given them up?' Edward asked.

'Yes,' said Cecil. 'George, the younger of the two, was seemingly planning to make his way here, but was taken from his London house in Blackfriars and conveyed directly to the Tower. There he has been most obliging in the naming of others in exchange for restraint on the part of those employed to obtain the truth.'

'So George Brooke and Markham were clearly intent on meeting up here,' Edward concluded. 'What pretence did they adopt — wishing to pay homage to our incoming monarch?'

'So Markham sought to pretend,' Cecil confirmed, 'but do you remember that I formerly advised you that he was banished from court? This was all the excuse I required to have him conveyed downstairs, there to put to him the rumours I had heard regarding his lack of fealty to Elizabeth's proclaimed heir. It proved all too easy to loosen his tongue, and he gave us the names of George and Henry Brooke. I have already been advised by those who serve me in the Tower that George has been obliging enough to reveal Henry's current location, and has provided other names.'

'The lady in Derbyshire?' Edward asked.

Cecil frowned. 'There is, as yet, little indication of what the conspirators had in mind, and even less regarding whether or not she had loaned her name to the plan, or given it her approval. Given that she is a full cousin to the incoming monarch, it would seem appropriate to give her the benefit of the doubt.'

'Sir Walter Raleigh?' Edward asked softly.

'George Brooke mentioned him, certainly, and I have not the slightest doubt that in the fullness of time he will emerge as the shadowy figure behind all of this. Not out of any Catholic sympathy, of course, but because he regards himself as a much more influential force behind matters at the English court. Remember I told you of a man called Baron Grey de Wilton? Did you hear any more about him during your brief time in Markham's company?'

'Not personally,' said Edward. 'You have news about him?'

'He might be expected to be a man most loyal to the new regime,' Cecil began. 'He is staunchly Protestant, to the point at which others of the true faith shun his extreme philosophies. He was also a bitter enemy of Essex, with whom he fell into dispute during their disastrous campaign in Ireland. He then transferred himself to the Low Countries, and at the urgent request of our late queen I sent Sir Henry Brooke and Sir Walter Raleigh to Ostend, in a bid to secure his assurances of loyalty to England. These I duly received, but it would seem that I was inadvertently responsible for the alliance that developed between the three of them. To my credit, it was Grey whose cavalry put a swift end to the Essex Rebellion, but by then the damage had been done.'

'Why would such a loyal subject — and a man with no love for Catholics — lend his support to a plot intended to place a rival Popish claimant on the English throne?' Edward asked.

'We do not know that this is his real motivation,' Cecil cautioned him. 'Indeed, to all outward appearances he welcomes James's accession to the English throne, to the extent that he was a member of the council that despatched me north to offer the crown to James. But seemingly he reacted adversely to the number of Scots noblemen that James has brought south with him, promising them high office. George Brooke was still smarting from his failure to obtain preferment from the late queen in relation to a certain prebend in Winchester, and it was he who introduced Grey to Markham. Markham, as already mentioned, had been banished from

Elizabeth's court, and in a fit of pique he was not prepared to honour her choice of successor. When you have three such bitter men seeking revenge, it is not long before their ambitions turn treasonous.'

'All this I can follow,' Edward replied, 'but where does it connect with Raleigh?'

'It does not, directly, so far as I have been able to ascertain,' Cecil admitted. 'In fact, I am inclined to believe that there is more than one treasonous plot. When I learned from Huntingdon, who in turn had been advised by you, of the possible raising of funds for an army of invasion sponsored by Spain, I concluded that treason on such a scale was beyond the mind of a fool like Markham. So, while Markham, Grey and George Brooke may have been plotting to perhaps kidnap James and ransom him in exchange for promises of better treatment of Catholics — in itself a preposterously bold scheme for dullards such as they — there would seem to be a darker, even bolder plot to raise an army in the name of Rome. It is this deeper plot that I suspect Henry Brooke of having become involved in, using his ongoing friendship with a certain Count of Arenberg, a Low Countries noble with close links with Spain. Arenberg is thick with Raleigh, and an offshore isle such as Jersey would be a highly convenient place for a vessel to land with a cargo of gold in order to finance a mercenary army.'

'With respect, Sir Robert,' Edward ventured, 'the bow against Raleigh would seem to be drawn exceedingly long.'

Cecil smiled unpleasantly. 'You are, of course, correct, which is why I am anxious for certain interrogators at my command to be given access to Henry Brooke, once he is captured and confined within the Tower. I will of course keep you fully informed of how matters progress, but for the moment I am instructed to pass on King James's grateful thanks for your bold and loyal efforts on his behalf, and wish you Godspeed back to your homes. In due course a tangible token of the king's gratitude may wing its way north, but for the time being you must be anxious to rejoin your families and return to your public duties.'

'We were dismissed rather quickly,' Francis observed the following morning as they began the long return journey north.

'We were no longer of any immediate use to him,' Edward replied. 'Have you not yet got the measure of how matters work in the highest circles?'

'I know more about apples than I do about courtly ways,' Francis admitted. 'Speaking of which, I wonder if we have become fathers again during our absence.'

'We will know within the week,' said Edward. 'However, I do not propose that we proceed back north with the same speed that we came south. Cecil handed me a substantial bag of coins shortly before we took our leave of him, and it may well be that we can find ample opportunity to spend it in the several inns that lie between us and Ashby.'

'What do you propose we do about Draycott and those of his following who made good their escape while we were being wrongfully arrested?' Francis asked bitterly.

Edward thought for a moment before replying. 'I know where they may all be found.'

'Even Draycott?'

'Especially Draycott. But up ahead I can see St Albans and dinner.'

'Do you think they will be welcoming?' Francis asked nervously as he and Edward trotted their mounts down the track that led to the Ashby dower house.

Edward chuckled and nodded ahead, to where Robbie Bishop was emerging from the dower house armed with a massive cudgel, no doubt alerted to their arrival by the sound of hooves on rough ground. Then he broke into a smile as he recognised them.

Once they had dismounted, Edward looked at Robbie's chosen weapon and asked, 'Does every would-be visitor to the castle get such an unfriendly welcome when they pass the dower house?'

'You *did* say to guard them well,' Robbie reminded him, 'and I have done.'

'Did either of the ladies deliver a child in our absence?' Francis asked eagerly.

Robbie nodded. 'Both of them.'

'And?' Edward prompted when the ensuing silence grew ominous.

'And what?' Robbie asked.

Francis let out a snort of exasperation. 'Are they all well?' he demanded.

'Yes, of course,' was Robbie's only reply.

Edward sighed heavily and persevered. 'The babies that were born to them — boys or girls?'

'One of each,' said Robbie.

It fell silent again before Francis intervened. '*Who* had *what*, you dumb lummox?'

'Can't rightly remember,' Robbie admitted, as both men pushed past him towards the house. On the porch they were met by a smiling Rose, who led the way into the main room, where Elizabeth and Kitty were seated at the dining table, each with an infant at her breast.

'Allow me to introduce Master Edwin Mountsorrel and Mistress Amy Barton,' Rose said as both mothers beamed a welcome at their homecoming men.

The celebration supper was not only a joyous one, but a masterpiece of the culinary arts. Both men proclaimed that it was the finest repast either had experienced since leaving Ashby almost two weeks previously.

'I should hope that what took me days to conceive, and hours to prepare, was indeed better that the swill they serve in country alehouses,' Rose replied. 'We've been anticipating your return with considerable enthusiasm, and once your latest offspring were safely delivered, there was nothing left for me to manage but banquet preparations ahead of your arrival home.'

'Except that it's not really "home", for any of us,' Elizabeth put in. 'How soon will the newborns be healthy enough for travel?'

'Whenever you are,' Rose told her, 'although you must ensure that you eat properly on your journeys, in order to keep up your supply of milk. I can obviously ensure that Kitty does, but Edward must put the welfare of you and your newborn son before anything else.'

'Believe me, he will,' Elizabeth insisted, then put her arm around Edward. 'So when can we leave here? Or is there something else you must do in order to save the nation before we can see our own hearth again?'

'I have thus far refrained from asking,' Rose chimed in, 'but how went your venture south?'

'Excellently well,' Edward assured her. 'Markham is in custody inside Theobalds House, Sir George Brooke is installed in the Tower, and the hunt is on for his brother Henry, Baron Grey de Wilton and even Sir Walter Raleigh, although Cecil remains uncertain regarding the part he has played in all this.'

'What about those awful fools who hung around Markham, and so badly abused every serving girl who had the misfortune to enter their part of Ollerton House?'

'They presumably entered Theobalds House as part of Markham's retinue,' Edward surmised. 'One must hope that they were captured along with him.'

'They were one less in number,' Francis added, despite the warning glare from Edward, 'because Edward killed him in a duel.'

'Another child on the way, the king's business to conduct, and you engaged in a *duel*?' Elizabeth demanded, outraged.

Edward shook his head. 'Francis wouldn't know a proper duel from a shovel. The man attacked me, so I was obliged to defend myself. It was the man calling himself de Vere,' he added, addressing Rose.

'It couldn't have happened to a more unworthy flapmouth,' she declared. 'But what of those simple but deluded people who were camped in Sherwood? Were they taken up also by Cecil's men?'

'No, they ran for their lives when they saw Francis and I being arrested. I have hopes that we can resettle them in such a way that they will at least fend off starvation.'

'So you were arrested?' Elizabeth probed with raised eyebrows. 'You failed to mention that.'

'It was all a misunderstanding,' Francis explained, 'and Cecil was most apologetic.'

'What do you mean by "resettle"?' Rose asked.

'They will shortly be opening an almshouse where the old St John's Hospital used to be,' Edward replied, 'or so my sheriffs advised me some weeks ago now. It's almost ready, and the poor and starving will be admitted there and given work in exchange for food, so hopefully they won't be coming into the town under the cover of night, and stealing what they need.'

Four days later Edward and his family said goodbye to Francis, Kitty, Rose and the two Barton children not long after their two wagons had crossed the River Trent by way of the Wilden Ferry, and their respective roads home diverged.

As Edward and Elizabeth arrived back at their house in Whitefriars Lane, they sensed that something was wrong. Edward turned the key in the lock of the heavy oak front door and realised that it had been left unlocked. Since Elizabeth had insisted that he make sure the door was firmly locked before they left, it was with growing apprehension that Edward nudged it open with his boot and quietly stepped inside, sword in hand, to survey the chaos that awaited them.

Either Nottingham had recently experienced an uncharacteristic storm, or someone had ransacked their home. Bedding, clothing, cushions and tableware lay strewn everywhere, smashed earthenware eating utensils lay in shards among the rushes, and someone had daubed crude insults on the plaster wall in what looked, and smelled, like horse dung. Elizabeth gave a sharp cry from behind him as she took it all in, then said, 'This is what happens to your home when you decide to play the part of the nation's hero, and abandon your family to its fate. Oh dear God, please no — not my best chest!'

Conspicuous by its absence was Elizabeth's pride and joy, a carved oak chest that had been a wedding present to her from her employer at the time, Sir Francis Willoughby. It had occupied almost one entire wall of their living room, and had been filled with items that Elizabeth held dear, such as childhood mementos and lacy garments. Edward felt the rage welling up within him, and was about to let fly a string of oaths, when he heard voices in the doorway behind him, and there stood their immediate neighbours, Tom Bradden and Will Gosling.

'We didn't dare stop them,' Tom told him with a crestfallen look, 'since they were armed with swords. They came a few days back.'

'Who's "they"?' Edward demanded.

'The bloke in charge of them said to tell you his name was Draycott, and that you'd asked for it,' Will replied.

'It's all right, both of you,' Edward reassured them. 'No-one's suggesting that you could have done anything to stop them, and at least I know who was responsible. I also know where he may be hiding, and was planning on paying him a visit anyway.'

18

Edward's original plan to resume his duties the following day was placed firmly in abeyance by Elizabeth's insistence that he remain at home to help with the restoration of the house. The next two days therefore consisted of picking up pieces of smashed crockery, burying the broken items in a deep pit in the garden behind the house, and listening to Elizabeth's tuts, groans, and tears as she discovered yet another missing memento.

She was also breast-feeding little Edwin, named after his grandfather in Ashby without any prior consultation with Edward. Her excuse was that the Earl of Huntingdon, upon being advised of the two recent births, had insisted on sending a local clergyman to conduct a joint baptismal ceremony in the absence of both fathers, ahead of which names had to be chosen. 'If you had taken the trouble to be there,' she said more than once, though he had made no complaints about the name given to his second son, 'you could have helped me choose a name more to your liking.' He quite liked 'Edwin', but there seemed to be little point in saying so.

Finally, on the third day since their return, he was grudgingly granted leave to go back to work. There were faint cheers as he appeared in the constabulary muster room in the Guildhall, where Senior Constable Durward formally welcomed him back, and assured him that the town had remained relatively quiet during his absence. Robbie Bishop had reported back for duty already, and had told his colleagues of Edward's journey south in the company of Francis Barton.

'You'll find it a bit quiet, after all that excitement in London,' said Durward.

Edward shook his head. 'I wasn't in London, exactly, and to be perfectly candid with you, a distinct lack of excitement would be very welcome right now. Apart from anything else, I have to meet with the sheriffs without delay, and then I have to investigate the burglary of my own house during my absence. Was it not reported?'

'Yes, it was — by a couple of your neighbours,' Durward told him. 'They even gave us a name.'

'That name being Draycott, I believe,' Edward replied.

'Yes, that's it. Ain't he the one who was bringing all the vagrants into town? There's not been sight nor sound of them lately, by the way.'

'That's because they were all inadvertently involved in the attempt on the king, thanks to Draycott,' Edward told him. 'They all slipped from our grasp, but I believe I know where to find him at least, once I've presented myself to the sheriffs and listened to their never-ending complaints.'

After fortifying himself with a mutton pie from the street vendor who plied his trade in Weekday Cross, immediately outside the Guildhall, Edward opted to make his first report to Sheriff Hynde. For one thing his townhouse, in Halifax Lane, was less distance to walk, and for another it was Hynde who seemed to be the more eager of the two to open the proposed almshouse, and Edward had a promise to keep.

'So you're back. And not before time,' said Hynde as he left Edward, as usual, standing before his desk in the small study to the rear of his house. 'We were fortunate that there was little crime in the town during your lengthy absence, and Secretary Cecil speaks highly of your efforts in ferreting out those who had treasonous ambitions against our new king. I have a despatch from him, in which he has entrusted me with a draft drawn on the deposits of Oliver Braintree, the goldsmith in Goose Gate. It is for a hundred pounds, and is yours to claim whenever you have the time. From what I have been advised by that senior constable of yours, you may wish to put it towards new furnishings for your house.'

'Yes, indeed,' said Edward, 'and Master Cecil, or Viscount Cranborne as he is now, is most generous. But might I enquire regarding the current state of your plan to open an almshouse in the old St John's Hospital?'

'It will be opening its doors next week,' Hynde beamed. 'We managed to reach an agreement on the appointment of its first overseer — a man called Bradbury. Once a few unfortunate souls find shelter under its roof, we can expect a noticeable reduction in the numbers sneaking into the town by night to engage in all manner of villainy.'

'If I were to round up a substantial number of them and bring them down to this new almshouse, I take it that this would meet with your approval?'

'Of course, but how do you intend to achieve that?'

'As you may be aware, I was once pretending to be one of their number. I believe they will trust me when I make the offer. Better that they come into town lawfully, with me, rather than unlawfully under the guidance of that dreadful man Draycott.'

'Will you be bringing him in as well?' Hynde asked.

'I will indeed, but not quite in a manner that he will appreciate.'

Although it was only late afternoon, The Partridge was already overcrowded with noisy drunks and the floor was awash with spilt ale and vomit. Eager town doxies grabbed at Edward's tunic as he moved towards the counter, behind which two men and a woman were handing out pots of ale.

'Take your place in the queue,' Edward was ordered by the older of the two men as he forced his way through the heaving throng to the front row.

'I don't need to,' Edward insisted, 'since I'm the town bailiff, and the terms of your licence from the magistrates require that you make the place available for inspection at all times.'

'So go away and do some inspecting,' came the rude reply.

'I'm looking for Nathaniel Brewer,' said Edward, keeping his eyes firmly on the faces of the other two behind the counter.

'Well, he ain't here,' the older man insisted.

Edward smiled knowingly. 'Which makes it all the more surprising that when I mentioned that name, both of your companions flicked their eyes in your direction. You're Nathaniel Brewer, aren't you?'

'I'm admitting to nowt,' Brewer insisted.

'I wasn't aware that you'd done anything wrong — not recently, anyway. But the magistrates will be informed of your willingness to play host to those entering the town illegally under the guidance of one Josiah Draycott. He's the one I'm really here to speak to.'

'Ain't seen him in weeks,' said Brewer, just as the woman who'd been handing out pots of ale slipped from behind the counter and disappeared into the back corridor.

'Well, I'll just wait here for a moment,' said Edward, 'until you and he can become reacquainted. By my calculation it requires only another minute or so before Mr Draycott comes back into your life somewhat dramatically.'

'Please yourself,' Brewer snarled as he returned to handing out pots of ale. He looked up in alarm shortly afterwards, when loud protests from a male voice became audible from the general area of the rear door. Robbie Bishop appeared, holding Draycott firmly, with one arm around his throat and one large hand across his crotch.

'Look who I found, trying to sneak out the back way,' Robbie called triumphantly. 'You were right, sir.'

'Get this tame bear of yours off me!' Draycott demanded.

'Perhaps, in a short while,' said Edward. 'First of all, tell me where you sold off that oak chest that you and your companions stole from my house.'

'Don't know what you're talking about,' Draycott insisted, then gave a scream of agony as Robbie tightened his grip on his testicles. 'No — wait! Hang on!'

Edward laughed. 'That's precisely what Constable Bishop will do if you don't reveal — *now* — where my furnishings have been lodged.'

'With Ben Barker — the carpenter in Bellar Gate!' Draycott said. 'Now for the love of God, get this brute off me!'

'In the fullness of time,' Edward promised. 'First he will deliver you to the Guildhall.' He nodded to Robbie as he added, 'Throw him in the filthiest, smelliest cell you can find, and have him charged with the attempted murder of the town bailiff. Then come back and meet me outside here with three more constables and a wagon.'

'Are you interested in a fine piece of furniture?' Ben Barker asked unctuously as he put down his chisel and walked through to the front of his workshop, where various items were awaiting sale.

'I have need of a fine oak chest,' Edward replied, 'one that has drawers in which my wife can store her most precious items.'

'Well, fortune has smiled upon you, my friend,' Barker told him. 'It just so happens that I have the very item in my workshop to the rear of here, if you'd care to step in there with me. Perhaps your companion would like to acquaint himself with some of our other items in the meantime,' he added with a nod in Robbie's direction.

In the rear workshop, Edward walked over to the oak chest that he knew so well. Along its lower panels it still exhibited some of the marks left by his children as they'd raced past it on their toy horses over the years. 'It's a fine piece,' he observed, 'but it appears to bear some marks of previous use.'

Barker appeared startled for a moment, but rapidly regained his composure. 'It's all the fashion these days, sir. The true gentry do not always wish to give the impression that their wealth has been recently acquired, and there is therefore a demand for items of furniture that exhibit signs of old age. I am skilled in the art of inflicting such marks on items that I have just completed, thereby making them of greater interest to the more discerning gentlemen such as yourself.'

'How do you contrive to make them look as if the sun has faded one side of them where they sat in a parlour somewhere?' Edward asked in pretended fascination, now beginning to enjoy himself.

Barker swallowed hard. 'I'm afraid that's an aspect of my art that makes my work unique, and much sought-after, so you will forgive me if I decline to give away a trade secret.'

'Of course,' Edward replied. 'How much will it cost me to acquire this unique piece?'

'For a gentleman of quality such as yourself, I am prepared to let it go for twenty pounds,' said Barker.

'Let us return to your front premises, there to discuss the terms under which I will acquire the item,' Edward suggested, then nodded briefly to Robbie as they re-entered the original room.

'You suggested that I might be a gentleman of some quality,' Edward went on as Robbie sidled silently up behind Barker, 'and indeed you are correct. I even have a title. I am the town bailiff of Nottingham.'

Barker's face paled.

'I have another entitlement that might well be of interest to you,' Edward added, 'namely the ownership of that oak chest that you stole, and just attempted to sell back to me. Take him in charge, Robbie.' Two strong arms encircled Barker from behind.

'I never stole it!' Barker insisted.

'Then tell me who did,' Edward demanded.

'A bloke called Draycott,' said Barker, gasping as Robbie's hold tightened.

'As I thought. Did he by any chance bring anything else in here at the same time?'

'No, just that — honest!'

'I'm prepared to believe you, and on this occasion the matter will be taken no further,' said Edward. 'But rest assured that these premises will be the first port of call when items such as mine are reported stolen in future. Now, you might wish to help the gentlemen waiting outside to lift the chest into the cart they have brought, so that I can return it to where it rightfully belongs.'

An hour later the cart had arrived at the house in Whitefriars Lane. Robbie Bishop and three constables took one corner each of the heavy chest and began walking it carefully towards the door that Elizabeth held open for them. She looked at Edward with raised eyebrows.

'Did you buy me a new one, and is this your way of getting back into my favour?'

'I opted to locate and retrieve your old chest rather than buying you a new one,' Edward replied. 'But yes, my aim is to get back into your favour.'

'Oh, you lovely man!' she all but cried as she hugged him. She lowered her voice. 'You'll learn the extent of my gratitude when the family are asleep.'

By the time that this long anticipated moment arrived, Elizabeth had learned to her delight that many of her prized possessions remained in the chest. Tears rolled down her face as she lovingly fondled several modest items of jewellery, an embroidered prayer book from her childhood, and the christening bonnets of Margaret and Robert. She then looked across at Edward after checking that Edwin was still asleep in his makeshift cot.

'Upstairs — now,' she whispered.

'I'd be delighted to oblige,' Edward told her, 'but don't make it last all night, because I must return to Sherwood on the morrow.'

19

The next morning, Edward rode to Francis and Kitty's orchard in Daybrook. He was at the head of a procession of four open wagons, each with a town constable on its front board.

'You're too early for the apple harvest,' Francis called out teasingly as he looked up from where he was sharpening a saw.

'We're heading for Sherwood,' Edward informed him.

'You won't find any apples there, either,' Francis joked, 'and I hope that you haven't invited your friends to dinner.'

'How many wagons can you supply, along with drivers?'

'Two, if you give me time to call in the Bestwood constable. Why?'

'Because, if you recall, I promised those unfortunate folk living rough in the forest that if they dispersed lawfully from their camp in Waltham Cross, I'd arrange for them all to be taken into the new Nottingham almshouse.'

'What I recall, since you put me to the task,' Francis replied, 'is that they didn't "disperse lawfully", as you put it. Instead, they fled like rabbits when the royal troops arrived, leaving you and I as the only ones available for arrest.'

'All the same, they didn't offer any resistance, and a promise is a promise. If you saw how they have to live, your heart would be overcome with compassion for them. Look at it another way: if they move out of Sherwood into the town in a lawful fashion, they won't be tempted to enter it by night, and your duties will be that much lighter.'

'There's that, I suppose,' Francis conceded, 'but you forget that the new almshouse is meant only for those residing in the town parishes — St Mary's, St Peter's and St Nicholas's. Sherwood is its own parish.'

'I'll confront that obstacle if anyone chooses to raise it,' said Edward, 'but for the time being I'd be obliged if you'd raise your Bestwood constable and join your two wagons to the line.'

'How do you know that they'll treat us graciously when we appear in their midst armed with wagons and constables?' Francis asked. 'Our last encounter was when you killed one of their number in front of their eyes. If they conclude, on first sight of us, that we're about to apprehend them, then we can expect to come under a hail of arrows, and being forest people they're likely to be very skilled in their use of bows.'

'I already considered that possibility,' said Edward, 'which is why the wagons will be left at the inn in Edwinstowe, where the men can be fed. Meanwhile, I'll go alone to the camp and assure them that they have nothing to fear, and everything to gain, by climbing into the wagons, which I'll come back to collect once they consent to that.'

'If you finish up with your head cut off, Elizabeth will not be best pleased,' Francis observed.

'Since I won't be available to blame, for once, that will be a further pleasure for you to look forward to,' Edward replied with a laugh.

Francis sighed. 'I had hoped that our recent journey south was the end of your seeming ambition to depart from this life, but never let it be said that I refused to come to your assistance. Get the wagons turned in the orchard back there, and give me a chance to hitch my two together behind the one horse. We'll pick up Constable Job Prentice on our way north, since Bestwood is little more than a mile out of our way. I still regard you as a man bereft of his wits, but then I've never known you to be anything else, and we're both still alive. May I tell Kitty that I'll be home for supper?'

Edward thought for a moment, then shook his head. 'By the time we have everyone transferred into the town, it will be dark, so supper will be at my house. You can depart from there at cock-crow tomorrow.'

Most of the camp's inhabitants looked up apprehensively as Edward trotted his mount into the clearing, and several reached for whatever crude weapons lay to hand. Then Janey walked out from her rough slab dwelling, a broad smile on her face.

'You've come back for that roll I promised you, have you? I heard you'd been arrested by the king's men, but here you are. D'you want summat to eat?'

'No thanks, Janey,' Edward replied. 'But I'd be grateful for some beer while you gather everyone around, so that I can tell them something very important about their futures.'

'For all we know, you've come to arrest the lot of us,' one man called out suspiciously.

'On my own?' Edward countered. 'I'm here to offer all of you a more secure future, that's all.'

'And why would you want to do that?' another man asked.

Edward had his reply ready. 'I lived among you for long enough to realise how difficult it is for you to feed yourselves, your women and your children. I can take you all into town with me lawfully, rather than you trying to sneak in under the cover of night. Once in town you'll be provided with a roof over your heads and regular supplies of food, in exchange for work. In the fullness of time you may even be able to move to a dwelling of your own, working for your own reward and providing for the futures of your children.'

'What happened to Master Draycott?' asked the same doubtful cynic who'd begun the questioning.

Edward was grateful for the opening. 'He was arrested by me three days ago. He'd been skulking in a filthy alehouse in town — the place that you would all have been taken to by him, if you'd made it into Nottingham.'

'What was he arrested for?' someone asked.

Edward's face took on a more serious expression. 'He tried to kill me. He and Sir Griffin Markham had me thrown into a pit under the flagstones of the north wing of Ollerton Hall, but I was rescued by that brave young man you chased out of here — the one calling himself Robbie Blythe. His real name is Robbie Bishop, and he's one of my constables.'

'So you really *are* a bailiff, like Master Draycott said?' his main interrogator demanded accusingly. 'And now you've come to arrest us all?'

Edward tutted in frustration. 'This conversation appears to be going round in circles. You have my word that I'm not here to arrest any of you. Instead I'm here to offer you all a better life, and with Draycott in prison it's the best offer you're likely to get. It's better than the one he promised you even when he *wasn't* in custody. But I'm getting tired of standing here, so if you can't see further than the ends of your noses, I'll just return to Nottingham alone. But ask yourselves this, before you reject my offer: why did Draycott and Markham try to kill me? What evil scheme were they involved in that I was about to unearth? Why would they kill a man sworn to uphold the law?'

It fell silent, until a woman's voice could be heard from near the back of the crowd.

'The bloke's got a point there. And how much longer are we going to stay in this hole, cold, hungry, filthy and living like the

187

lowest of animals? I'm prepared to take this man's word, even if I'm the only one. I've got nowt to lose, and anything's got to be better than this.'

The swell of voices raised in sympathy with this reasoning soon reached a clamorous level. With a sigh of relief Edward began organising the forest dwellers into family groups before riding off, returning shortly afterwards with the wagons into which almost everyone was loaded. The few who remained turned their backs disdainfully on those who had taken up Edward's offer. Edward was concerned to note that one of them was Janey, who stood at the door to her hut with her children, giving him a sad farewell wave as a tear rolled down each cheek.

The procession came to a halt outside the locked gates of the almshouse as Edward raised a hand, then dismounted and walked towards the defiant man who was standing with the gate keys in his hands.

'I got your message,' the man told Edward. 'I'm Thomas Bradbury, the recently appointed overseer. As I understand it, you were intending to bring people from the county to enjoy the benefits of a charitable institution intended only for those from the town parishes.'

'I was not brought up to believe that charity comes with territorial boundaries,' Edward replied sternly as Francis came to stand beside him. 'Bailiff Barton here, being from the county, can give you ample evidence of the suffering of these people.'

'I can only advise you,' Bradbury insisted, 'that the financial provision for those who enter this establishment comes from those charitably minded worthies of the town who donate a portion of their wealth. They are pledged to do so only for the less fortunate within their own parishes. However worthy may be the cause of those you have brought here, they are not from any of our three parishes.'

'Is it solely a matter of finance?' Edward asked.

Bradbury shook his head. 'It is also a matter of the limited accommodation. The almshouse in its present situation can provide for only a hundred or so deserving souls. How many are behind you?'

'Sixty at most,' Edward replied. 'How many have you in there at present?'

'Twenty,' said Bradbury.

'So were these good folk to be granted admission, you would, by my calculation, still have room for twenty or so more? And you have acquired only twenty from the local parishes in the few weeks that you've been open?'

'We do not have financial provision for sixty additional souls, without inflicting on those who pay my stipend a most grievous additional tax.'

'How much is the estimated cost for each one admitted through your gates?' Edward asked.

'A pound a head.'

Edward reached inside his jerkin. 'So, in order to admit sixty, if we ignore for the moment where they have come from, you would require a charitable donation of sixty pounds. Have I got that right?'

'You have.'

Edward produced, with a flourish, the document that he'd extracted from his jerkin. 'I have here a draft drawn upon the credit of Secretary of State Viscount Cranborne. It may be presented at the premises of the goldsmith Oliver Braintree in Goose Gate.' Then he stepped forward and lowered his voice as he added, 'I shall not be seeking anything further from it.'

Bradbury's eyes widened in amazement as he realised that he was being offered not only the estimated cost of admission of every person in Edward's party, but also what amounted to a bribe of forty pounds — almost four times his annual stipend. The temptation was too great.

An exhausted cheer went up as the gates were unlocked, and Edward and Francis stood to one side and wished the new residents good fortune as they entered the almshouse. The wagons, with their attendant constables, reappeared within minutes, and as they all dispersed to their homes, Francis drew Edward to one side.

'That draft from Cecil — how much was it for?'

'A hundred pounds,' Edward informed him.

Francis let out a muted oath. 'You were guilty of bribing a public official.'

'Correct, and he was guilty of accepting it. I am now in a position to blackmail him in the future, should the cause be worthy enough to risk my own dismissal from office for revealing what just took place.'

'Why should I not arrest you now?'

'Because I know you too well, Francis, and I saw the look of pity in your eyes when you saw how those poor wretches were living. To arrest me would require you to have them removed from the almshouse and cast back out into the countryside, from where they would plague you nightly with their attempts to re-enter the town.'

'You devious devil,' Francis muttered as he reached inside his own jerkin and extracted a document, which he handed to Edward. 'You can have mine, since you gave away your own. You are not the only one who was rewarded by Cecil.'

'How much is it for?' Edward asked as he peered at it in the rapidly fading light.

'Twenty pounds only,' Francis complained, 'but it's better than nothing, I suppose, and you were the one who took all the risk.'

'This is true,' Edward agreed, 'which is why I will accept it, if only to enable Elizabeth to replace those items of our kitchenware that were smashed or stolen during the burglary. However, we still have enough left to be able to offer you a hearty supper. Just don't tell Elizabeth that I gave away twice that amount. I'm only recently back in her favour.'

A NOTE TO THE READER

Dear Reader,

Thank you for investing your valuable reading time in this, the fifth novel in the Bailiff Mountsorrel Tudor Mystery series, this time set early in the reign of James I. It was a period of considerable potential for historical novelists.

The death of Elizabeth I created a succession crisis for England, given her resolute refusal to name her heir during the years in which she'd been in fading health. At her bedside as she approached her final breath was Robert Cecil, her Secretary of State, and the son of Baron Burghley, the man who'd steered her through her difficult years, particularly when she herself inherited the throne unexpectedly on the death of her half-sister Mary.

It was Cecil's assertion, which no-one was in a position to refute, that when he'd leaned in closely to hear her response to his question regarding whether or not she wished the English Crown to go to James VI of Scotland, she'd smiled and drawn an imaginary crown around her own head as a symbol of her consent. It made dynastic sense, since the two of them were related through their common ancestor Henry VII. It was also a vindication of the negotiations that Cecil had secretly been conducting with James, during trips to Edinburgh designed to ensure that Cecil would enjoy pre-eminent favour if James succeeded Elizabeth.

But there was another person related to Elizabeth in the same degree, namely Lady Arbella Stuart, James's cousin. Their respective fathers had been brothers, so whatever degree of kinship James had with Elizabeth could also be claimed by

Arbella, who lived in relative obscurity on the Derbyshire estate of her grandmother, the notoriously wealthy and ambitious Bess of Hardwick.

A dark horse she might be in the succession race, but for a significant group within the England that Elizabeth left behind, she had one irresistible advantage — she was Catholic, by upbringing and preference.

The religious wars that had threatened to tear England apart during almost the entire Tudor period were not yet fully extinguished. Although Elizabeth had, in her later years, been obliged to stamp hard on the remaining adherents of the Roman Church who had hatched one plot after another against her, the era when Catholicism had been the national religion under 'Bloody Mary' was still within living memory. The Protestant purge against closet Catholics that had been relentlessly pursued by Elizabeth's advisers, chief among whom had been the Cecils, had not entirely eliminated the scheming for a return to Rome by those who looked askance at the proposed accession of the avowedly Protestant James.

But those opposed to the continuation of a Protestant monarchy were bitterly divided. The traditionally 'hardline' Jesuits whose priests had been hounded by the Cecils' spymaster, Walsingham, had now opted to keep a lower profile, and their spiritual leader in England, John Gerard, and his acolyte, Father Henry Garnet, were opposed to any violent uprising that might further blacken the Catholic image and lead to ongoing persecution. This was not to the liking of another group of practising Catholics that contained among their number ordained priests who were not members of the Jesuit Order. They were labelled 'secular priests', and they had the support of various nobles who, while not necessarily inspired by a desire for the restoration of Rome as the spiritual foundation of the English Church, had various reasons for rejecting the incoming King of Scotland as the person to whom they must swear allegiance.

It is this latter group who feature in my novel, and they began hatching plots. Not just one single plot that would ensure that all their efforts were concentrated on one master plan, but two power grabs that co-existed, and contained conspirators common to both. The one you have just read about became known as the 'Bye Plot', principally because it was secondary to a more fundamental 'Main Plot'.

Sir Griffin Markham; Henry Brooke, the eleventh Baron Cobham; his younger brother George Brooke; and Thomas Grey, the fifteenth Baron Grey de Wilton, conceived the 'Bye Plot' under which James of Scotland was to be seized and held to ransom in exchange for concessions being granted to practising Catholics, most notably freedom of worship and the removal of the fines to which those of their faith were subjected. When they unwisely sought the approval and support of the Jesuit faction, it was John Gerard himself who set in motion a process by which the plot was revealed to Robert Cecil ahead of its execution, and fizzled out ignominiously when the leaders unwisely presented themselves at the Cecil home, Theobald House.

The interrogations that followed revealed the 'Main Plot', which was intended to remove James from the throne completely and replace him with Arbella Stuart. Henry Brooke was denounced by his own brother George in what proved to be a futile bid to save his own neck, and it rapidly emerged that the funds for this uprising were intended to come from Spain, through the intermediary hands of Sir Walter Raleigh, then Governor of Jersey. Their fates lie outside the scope of this novel, but they were not good. However, since it was not known for certain whether Arbella Stuart had even been aware of this plot hatched in her name, still less whether or not she had consented to it, she was not put on trial, but eventually died in the Tower anyway when she married a man reputed to have designs on James's throne.

One of the ironies of all this was that the England they were all seeking to rule was by no means a great prize. Gone was the splendour of the Elizabethan court, the English navy's dominance of the high seas, the flow of riches from pirate activities by the likes of Drake and Hawkins, and the security of English trade across the Channel. By 1603 the nation had endured appalling weather, cataclysmically poor harvests, and an economic downturn that had made paupers out of previously wealthy men. This 'Dearth', as it was known, was exacerbated by chronic unemployment, notably among those who had served Elizabeth in her army and navy, only to be cast back into the general workforce without a pension, without the offer of work, and in many cases without limbs. They formed a social substrata popularly known at the time as the 'sturdy beggars', and they were a menace to those travelling the highways. Even the less aggressive of them were considered a threat to the peace of the nation with their constant pleas for alms.

It was in response to this issue that the first 'Poor Laws' were enacted. They had as their primary focus the relief of poverty by means of a levy on the wealth of the more fortunate in society, organised on a parish basis. This would, centuries later, evolve into the infamous 'workhouse' system, but initially it seems to have been the somewhat patronising intention of those who initiated the scheme that the deserving poor should be fed and housed in return for work that would generate income for the poorhouse to which they'd been admitted, thereby relieving the burden on those who were being taxed in order to finance the system.

There were two inherent flaws in this method of poor relief that rapidly became evident, and are referred to in this novel. The first was the predictable reluctance of the wealthy to be further taxed for what they regarded as subsidising idleness, and the second was that the entire initiative was organised on a parish basis. This placed a sometimes intolerable burden on a relatively poor urban parish with a high percentage of unemployed, while leaving some rural parishes without any relief at all. This is why I felt the need to draw attention to what must have been large swathes of the countryside burdened with desperate and starving former land workers who might be tempted to resort to highway robbery, cut-pursing and the like. Groups just like the huddled families within Sherwood Forest, living lives not dissimilar to the mythical Robin Hood of a past century, but without his romantic and humanist traits.

The main characters within these pages — Edward, Francis and their families — are of course fictional, as indeed is Josiah Draycott, although no doubt men like him exploited the poor in the manner suggested. But the supporting cast — Cecil, the Brooke brothers, Markham, Grey, Raleigh and Arbella Stuart — really existed, and largely performed the actions I've described.

As always, I look forward to reading your reviews on either **Amazon** or **Goodreads**, or you can contact me directly on my author website: **davidfieldauthor.com**.

Happy reading!

David

Sapere Books is an exciting new publisher of brilliant fiction and popular history.

To find out more about our latest releases and our monthly bargain books visit our website:
saperebooks.com

Printed in Great Britain
by Amazon